T0035485

Mahuldiha Days

Mahuldiha Days

ANITA AGNIHOTRI

translated from the original Bengali by
Kalpana Bardhan

zubaan

ZUBAAN
128 B Shahpur Jat, 1st Floor
New Delhi 110 049
Email: contact@zubaanbooks.com
Website: www.zubaanbooks.com

First published in English by Zubaan Publishers Pvt. Ltd 2018
Previously published as part of *Forest Interludes*, Kali for Women
Published in Bengali as *Mahuldihar Din*, 1996

10 9 8 7 6 5 4 3 2 1

ISBN 978 93 85932 17 5

Zubaan is an independent feminist publishing house based in New Delhi
with a strong academic and general list. It was set up as an imprint of
India's first feminist publishing house, Kali for Women, and carries
forward Kali's tradition of publishing world quality books to high editorial
and production standards. *Zubaan* means tongue, voice, language, speech
in Hindustani. Zubaan publishes in the areas of the humanities, social
sciences, as well as in fiction, general non-fiction, and books for children
and young adults under its Young Zubaan imprint.

Typeset in Baskerville 11/14 by Jojy Philip, New Delhi 110 015
Printed and bound at Replika Press Pvt. Ltd, India

Translator's Introduction

Anita Agnihotri (born Chattopadhyay in 1956 in Kolkata) was still a relatively young but highly regarded writer when she published this novel in 1996. It is important to remember the period she wrote about in this novel, the eighties, concerning her early career as a civil servant, and the sixties, through seventies, concerning her childhood and adolescence. That by no means is to make the novel seem dated, socio-politically speaking or culturally. Not only because in many ways things basically have not changed all that much. But because it is a novel, a novel woven out of the material of a singular life in first person, a person deeply sensitive to the society, culture and nature surrounding her at each stage of her life. The novel's structure is at once imaginative and involved in a highly engaging manner, it is a fine work, both as literature and as social commentary at the interface of gender, politics and administration. And it is a novel of stark realities mingling with poetic images that took this translator quite some time to get across just so.

An IAS officer since 1980 (risen from assignments as district magistrate to a secretary to the Ministry of Social Justice & Empowerment) Anita is also an economist with

post-graduate degrees from Calcutta and East Anglia
universities, and a poet who has published from childhood
(starting with the children's magazine Sandesh, founded and
edited by Satyajit Ray). Her substantial literary production,
comprising fiction, essays and poetry, is much appreciated
not only by her mostly Bengali readers, but also translated
into English, German, Swedish and major Indian languages,
by non-Bengali readers. Her readership and popularity is
especially wide among the younger generations interested in
social activism and the political mechanics of a democratic
'new' India still struggling with prejudice and hierarchies.

Working as a district magistrate and administrator of
rural development, she had direct experience of many of the
poorest tribal areas of Orissa and east-central India generally.
And by marriage (to Satish, also an IAS officer whom she met
as a fellow trainee at Shimla) she is also closely connected
with cultures and customs of Maharashtra and western India
generally. Although intensely Bengali in her literary tone and
idiom, she is a truly modern all-India writer, whose work
springs as much from literary imagination and life experience
in a country at once modern and traditional as from close
knowledge of socio-cultural contexts of the stories she tells.

The aspects of her storytelling – literary sensibility, an
administrator's professional experience, social analysis skills, a
willed commitment to social justice, and the life of a working
mother and wife – combined to produce a unique literary
voice that rings true and urgent, and resonates with humanism
and feminism. The artist's voice is also that of an activist who
has held offices of power and authority, functioned within
the hierarchic and departmentalized arena of the Indian
Administrative Services. The novel depicts a maturation of
perspective through involvement and struggles within an

often conflictual process of modernization of a stratified rural India. Its strength comes from the writer's image-artistry, evocative language, grasp of sociology and administrative matters, and the life of one passionate about her family and the people she is charged with to help and govern. Not a common mix. Her narrative effectively manages to override the usual separation between fiction and non-fiction, between literature and journalism. This is what makes this novel both relevant and readable. The authorial voice is urgent, astute, and exuberant, the tone free of abstraction and pretension.

In Bengal, the combination of a writer who is also a district magistrate has a daunting parallel in the towering figure of Bankimchandra Chattopadhyay. The indisputable progenitor of the novel in Bengal's, as also the subcontinent's vernacular literature, his fiction is matched in influence by his work as essayist and social philosopher, his razor-sharp analysis of contemporary society and economy. But he kept these two sides of his writing mostly separate. Both as novelist and as essayist, he kept a deliberate distance between his private life and life as a civil servant. An imperiously private man, he never wrote and published anything that could be construed as directly or implicitly autobiographical; his essays are didactical. Even the narrative voice in his satirical Kamalakanta's Journals is distanced from 'his own by a series of symbolic disjunctions'.[1] No main character of his novels resembles himself or any aspect of his sparsely documented personal life. By his temperament and by the convention of the time, he remained implacably a private person.

Half a century later, Rabindranath Tagore in his fiction and non-fiction put a much greater charge of personal emotions and glimpses of the private self. This had to do with his poetic temperament, but partly also with the heady creative atmosphere within the Tagore clan. Had he not produced so much in poetry and autobiography (including personal letters), the personal might perhaps have figured in his fiction to an even greater extent. However, the presence of personal life in Tagore's fiction and essays came distilled with careful control. His perfection of artistic and psychic balancing still remains unmatched, perhaps because change of time and convention undercut his kind of filtering in literary work. Filtering out the first-person singular is no longer valued much as good taste or prized as artistic refinement. Instead, self-exposure is everywhere in fiction. Even in non-fiction, the energy of the personal essay is increasingly favoured over didactic reasoning and abstract phrasing. Even so, late-twentieth-century literature does not exactly abound in original exercises in the artistry of balancing the personal and the socio-political.

The blending of the private/autobiographic and the public/social in this novel, so unlike Bankimchandra, is not at all surprising. He belonged to mid-nineteenth-century colonial India, she to the late-twentieth-century India of career women. One, a major early figure of the Bengal Renaissance, the other an upcoming writer finding her niche in a bustling, thriving literary scene, exposed to cosmopolitan trends and lifestyles. One an aloof patrician reticent about private life, using different personal and social voices, the other a vibrant, middle-class woman juggling professional and family duties, mixing private and social thoughts.

Going beyond this, however, Anita melds fictional and documentary narratives to explore multiple layers of reality, hers and others. Freely moving back and forth between personal memory, professional experience, and a keen sense of history as well as folkloric collective memory, she delivers something that challenges and stimulates. One wants to go on reading, for the spontaneous humanism of how she lets the personal and the social mingle, lets facts and fiction, data and dreams, weave. Yet, her narrative style is far from the no-holds-barred self-dumping in the mass market. Though unregulated by Bankimchandra's standard, it is chaste by today's standard. Unlike Bankimchandra, unlike even Rabindranath, and unlike earlier generations of Bengali women writers, very little is veiled, encoded and so in need of decoding. Instead, we find her freely attempting to connect and converse, reflect on shared thoughts, resolve turmoil. And this she does without any resort to gratuitous graphic description or language.

'Narrative techniques are, after all, not ends in themselves but a means of achieving certain effects. We cannot know what a narrative is except in relation to what it does,'[2] the emotional response it calls up in the reader. The narrative technique that Anita has used in this novel, mixing journalistic accounts and poetic imagery, has an evocative quality that works to place her as a sociologist's writer and a writer's sociologist.

This novel, at one level, is a bildungsroman; a woman in her early thirties during a crisis in her personal and professional life, a crisis that leads to a passage towards maturity. Amidst the turmoil in family life and struggles in her profession, she retraces her passage through childhood and early youth. She has an intensely visual way of reliving her lived life – the neighbourhood park that was the lonely child's favourite haunt (though late in being sent to school she was secretly a precocious reader and writer); the unruly river in a tribal area of hills and forests where a posting took her amidst a wrenching family situation; and the bleakness of the lives of the marginalized people she is placed in charge of, but is depressingly unable to help in the face of stonewalling and departmental barriers. Signalled by the Calcutta park (the disorienting sorceress of her lonely childhood), and the Gurupriya river (the sun-drenched beauty of her galvanizing epiphanies of adulthood), she relives the crises of passage, the various stages of her struggles, through traumas minor and major, to integrate and reintegrate her private and social selves towards livable wholeness. The nitty-gritty details of everyday life and the minute perception counterpoint the stream-of-consciousness recounting of the process, the two harmonized by the lyrical language and vivid imagery (which made my work challenging enough).

At another level, the novel is a set of accounts of the cogs and wheels of development administration, the ins and outs of the system, the mechanics of encounters between officials and the people administered. The variables and contingencies of those interactions defy generalization but come out in stories.

At yet another level, the novel is a study in 'the soul of a professional administrator'. The phrase is not an oxymoron, and it should not signal snickers. Else, we should lose sleep over the thousands of young men and women – intelligent, educated, hard-working, well brought up – who genuinely aspire to a career in civil service, and not just as a job. While translating this novel, I could imagine the gleams of recognition in the eyes of both aspiring and established administrators as well as of the many for whom the issue of codes governing an administrator's soul remains open, far from closed.

KALPANA BARDHAN
February 2018, Berkeley

Notes

1. 'Bankim is staidly respectable, Kamalakanta is marginal, of doubtful occupation...a opium-eater; Bankim is a solid civil servant, a salaried man of a decidedly upper bracket; [Kamalakanta] is dependent on a mixture of something between respect and pity; Bankim is a realist. [Kamalakanta] is a dreamer...a bundle of negative attributes,...idle, disorderly, unmarried, unkempt,...everything that Bankim is not,...[yet] he is his self which has broken the syntax of reality, his self in a dream.' Sudipta Kaviraj. 1998. *The Unhappy Consciousness: Bankimchandra Chattopadhyay and the Formation of Nationalist Discourses in India*. Delhi: Oxford University Press. P. 28.

2. Philip Lopate (ed.). 1994. 'Introduction' in *The Art of the Personal Essay*. New York: Anchor Books, p. xxix.

1

To this day, I haven't been able to forget that river. Sometimes, when the cavern of mid-day silence is shattered by the sudden call of a bird—*torr-r torr-r,* or a whirl of wind smelling of the hot sun spirals towards the centre of the sky, a black butterfly, flitting in from nowhere, touches the gloom of the termite-infested mango tree for an instant, to disappear into the shaggy patch of darkness under a plum bush—it comes back to me. Perhaps then, in the gunj market below my half-open window, yet another day has closed in like a venomless snake head on the morning's trade. Only the wholesalers' bustle now, out-of-state dealers loading rows of trucks, flies buzzing over heaped-up rotting leaves, dust motes rise up clinging to the shafts of sunlight like lint.

At just such an hour, out of nowhere, that enchantress appears before me, overflowing the banks of a discoloured sky; her sun-splashed waters flash before my entranced eyes, the yellow-ochre sandbar. As though all the time she were here, right before my eyes, hidden by a sleight of hand in the shuffling of day and night scenes. Then I come to realize that this river, this sun-scented beauty, has me bound in her million spells. I've actually left her realm long ago—but she won't let me go, not easily! The four doors of her magic arena closing around me, she drowns me at the day's end in the maze of her blurry mirror.

So many times at midnight, or even later, her hypnotic call has followed me in pale moonlight. Etched against the sky is the city's silhouette, the halogen lights strong enough to dull the stars. A baby crow in the neem tree overhead caws in its sleep. Then, all of a sudden, like a tune drifting from afar, she comes and lodges in my bloodstream and refuses to let go. At once, wiping off the geometry of the city's night-body appears that blue-gray firmament stretching to the horizon. Instantly, eager stars in their thousands begin to shine in the mind's eye and, shivering at the unreal call of nightbirds atop the forest, I look up. There she is, spanning the horizon, the bandit woman—the sound of her laughter rings out in darkness! Yet in reality, I haven't seen her in a long time.

For so many years I've been wandering by myself away from that yellow and green of plateaus and hills covered with saal trees. Wandering, looking for an exit, just an easy-to-open plain green door in a white wall. Now and again with a start, I run my fingers over my face: has it turned into a mask? Wandering beyond the dusty town and its markets, listening at duskfall to the sound of conchshells blowing, I walk past rows of familiar faces to stand at the edge of a group of people, their faces lit by a gasoline lantern, yet no one recognizes me. Even then, in the depths of that weariness, I have felt her presence. This river, following a twisted yet insistent path, has kept up with me, hovering at the edge of my consciousness and never letting me out of her sight. Maybe it amuses her tonight to suddenly flash thus against the city backdrop. Perhaps she has decided to remind me of that evening, when I was looking absently for the light at the landing ghat.

'Where did the ghat's light go?'

The darkness absorbed my question the way the sea does.

Tonight, three souls in three quiet corners of the world are pulling at my mind in different ways. In my bedroom in Mahuldiha, almost swimming in the large bed, Kuki, has sensed that no car horn will sound in the portico tonight. First two and then all of her fingers in her mouth, she's now studying the irregular crisscrosses on the ceiling. Basumati sits on the floor by the bed, singing to Kuki in her native tongue, and patting her gently with her old roughened hands. Slowly Kuki will grow very quiet, until at one point deep sleep will come and abruptly touch her eyelids; she won't have me with her tonight. Once she's asleep, Basumati, will turn out the lights, leaving just the blue night light on. She'll unroll the mat on the floor, pull her thick wrapper over herself and put her head down to sleep.

In Swarupnagar down in the plains, six hundred kilometres and almost ten hours' journey from here, in a small whitewashed house, in bed in his own room Guddu is thinking of me. On his chest lies a slim book, open face-down. He has school at nine in the morning. Having asked him to go to sleep several times, Ranjan must be in the next room reading a newspaper. Guddu takes the bolster in his arms, puts a leg over it and breathes in its smell. Even from here I can tell he doesn't like it. Still, for a while he absently talks to the pillow. Occasional, stray words come to me, get in my eyes like windblown specks. Guddu, that is Swapno, will not have me there, not tonight, not tomorrow, not for several months now, not until the work of the development projects gets well under way: exactly when that will be is impossible to tell now.

Is Ranjan Srivastava thinking of me at this moment tonight? Perhaps he is, yet perhaps he doesn't realize he is. Under his tight, thin lips his heart is opaque as the network of veins is visible under his fair skin. Perhaps in his mind he turns over the memories of earlier days, one after another, plays with them with perfect ease, then puts them back in a darkened recess. I know Ranjan still loves me, even though he hasn't said it in a long time. Loves me, yet doesn't want me to feel his love in my heart or receive it in my body Amazing! Ranjan's passion is as mild as the scent of his aftershave, almost imperceptible, and totally disciplined. In my mind's eye, I see him get up. Switching off the television that was on at low volume, he goes to the door of Guddu's room and parting the curtain a bit, asks softly, 'Guddu, aren't you feeling sleepy yet?'

'Yes I am', Guddu firmly closes his eyes to convince Ranjan.

The house is on elevated ground, a mound of sorts; around it a scattering of other houses. Almost a full-scale colony. The town lights are sparkling below, along the geometric pattern of the roads. Ranjan, I can almost see you come out on the verandah, stand there.

Far away, I stand by this river, an immense open-winged sky over me. I, Babli, Kamalika Mukherji Srivastava. Tomorrow morning I've an inspection in Kumardihi. Tomorrow evening I'll be back in Mahuldiha. As I go on day by day, the future opens slowly ahead of me, like a carpet unrolling bit by bit, while behind me looms what seems like a frosted glass wall. Looking back, I can't clearly see anything.

Here the sky of the night world is filled to the brim with the rain's moist fragrance. If the moon were out, its light on the tenth waxing night would surely have draped the massive shadowy body of the forest in dreams. The sky has scattered

clouds now, no moon. The wet wind whistles lightly on its
way to the forests farther away. The forest on the right side is
tightly woven, the riverbank there the height of at least two
men. By daylight, one can see the water's teeth eating away
at the red soil steadily like a turtle. After the heavy rain, the
roiling muddy water reached the massive roots of the trees on
the bank's edge. Are there times when the trees worry that, on
a rainy day, the shoreline may give way and their bodies wash
away in a flood of yellow water? The thick forest on the right
marks the outer boundary of this subdivision.

The sprawling Jarangloi area is like a decapitated body,
its head cut off by this sabre of sharp-edged water. The trees
at least don't have to run households and tend to seasonal
chores surrounding the act of living, as the people do. Along
the opposite bank, on a patch of eroded ground, the people
who live in the row of mud huts belong to the untouchable
community of Khamarpara. At the crack of dawn, after
eating water-soaked leftover rice with chilli and onion, they
stand at the bend of the road to Khamarpara, hoping to be
hired for a day's wage. At the same bend of the road some time
after dusk, the contractor's truck returns and disgorges their
dusty bodies ravaged like sugarcane bagasse. Coming home
in the dark, groping in the blackness of their homes without
kerosene to light a lamp, they find the clay pot containing the
dregs of mahua or rice liquor. No matter if there's any of the
morning's rice still left soaking or if their wives have cooked
any, they pull a date-leaf mat to lie on and, barely listening
to the cries of hungry or sick children they sink into a deep
sleep, oblivious of what awaits them next morning.

Where I am now, the forest had set out its strands many
decades ago, the formations grown sparse now in the losing
battle with man. Dotted haphazardly along the sides of the

footpath stand a few tall arjun, gambhar, shimul trees, and a clump of neem. A lot of neem berries must have blown here at the start of the century. The wet path underfoot, in disrepair, slopes down to the water. The sound of the river is clearly audible through the darkness. It's the start of Sravan; the springs up in the Kaluaburhan hill to the north must be full. Like pythons waking from long sleep, they plunge unhurriedly into the river below. Straight ahead from this ghat, in the midst of the flooded river are the three huge rocks—Budroo, Jhumroo and Kattan—like baby elephants. Who gave them their names and when? Maybe two girls, inseparable friends from the Oraon neighbourhood, paddling across in the dry season's waist-deep water on their way home, named those rocks on a whim and went off laughing. Now the swift thrusts of water there have created a heart-stopping current. Even in daytime ferryboats cross at a respectful distance from those three rocks lurking like crocodiles—instead of cutting straight across, they make a long detour either left or right. Caught in this eddy, even a seasoned swimmer will go under, head smashed against the water's roaring laughter—the way Latif's boat overturned last year in the month of Asarh. After struggling with the current for a long time the marketplace folk swam ashore, wives and daughters out to sell fish and vegetables, with babies, and some school kids. Wet from head to toe, their cloth bags lost in the water with books, notebooks, pens and all, the kids were crying, inconsolable! But at least they survived, though that was only because a trained army guard, Karam Singh, happened to be in the boat. Like an otter diving under and coming up with fish, he desperately kept on, pushing one child at a time close to the bank and pressing back again to the whirlpool. The crowd collected that day on the river's right bank pointing fingers at the half-finished bridge and cursing. Why shouldn't they? Nine years, and the work on the bridge is still not complete. The main structure somehow got finished, then the pillars were made, one at a time with difficulty—but it took four years to get the land released from the forest department's grip. As a result, the approach road has not been constructed so far. The cagelike framework of the bridge hangs like an apparition over the swollen river. In an area where every little thing from matches to homeopathic pills comes in a boat, business is brisk for boatowners and building contractors, while the people have to depend for their survival on scraps of mercy doled out by those very chaps. Rumours are rife that the bridge is not getting finished just so that the contractor can stay in business. He has set up a thriving business in a shed by the riverside—the boat is his, the ferry service as well. It's leased for a year, and he's not letting go before the year is over. Not until he has separated the last wornout paisa from the loincloth waistfold of these shirtless skin-and-bones men!

I've seen this river downstream also, close to the estuary. One night I had to go across the river near Nuapathar at a late hour. The bridge was wide enough. I don't know what got into me, I had the jeep wait at the near end of it and crossed its entire length on foot. It was just past full moon; the blend of moonlight and the smell of water spread like vines over my whole body. Standing at the exact centre of the bridge, leaning over and looking at the pregnant water flow—it was like a strange conversation. The star-studded sky looked on with a thousand eyes; the river seemed asleep in the embrace of the two forest-covered banks, her face pressed in the stretch of white sand. Maybe, close to the ocean, a river becomes calm and quiet like this, bashful almost, in anticipation of union with the beloved. Yet, far up north here, she's a restless dancer, with so many bends and dark waters, so seductive, Gurupriya! Who could have given her this name? Ong, Tel, Jonk—these too are rivers. Somehow those names remind you of yellow-beaked shaliks hopping in the mud of the riverbank. But this enchantress is like a wide-eyed woman in a saffron sari, its free end blowing in the wind, and the sky and the wind playing with her long wavy hair. Each time I come near the bangle-tinkling sound of her lapping water I ask, under my breath, 'Who gave you this name?' And in response each time, a giggle runs across the ripples to the other bank, like an invisible violin's bow across its strings.

Though it's the month of Sravan, a pale sandbar still stays up like an open eye between two slick dark streams. It has smooth pebbles strewn on it: red, blueish ochre, with minute designs drawn on them by the water. So many times, kneeling by the water's edge, I've filled my sari's pallu with a selection to take along—for Guddu to play with. Guddu hasn't lost a single one, saved them neatly in his old tin suitcase. Stored in our Mahuldiha home in a corner of the inner veranda, along with his other treasures. After each visit he leaves his things behind, I don't know why, never takes any of them to Swarupnagar.

Right across from here, on the opposite bank, is a gigantic tamarind tree. Hundreds of white storks sleep, wings folded, in the tree at night. The leafy top looks almost white with them. Any sudden noise makes some of them flap their wings and move about the tree with half-awakened eyes. A faint smell of ordure pervades the air underneath. Even so, Sanatan stops the car there to wait for me, because it is right next to the boat landing. He's supposed to turn on the headlights to let us know he's arrived. From here, though, there's no sign of that light. Perhaps the car is not there yet.

In this eroded, uneven high bank not far from the forest,
hidden in the dark somewhere very close, Bishai Munda waits
with his boat. By boat I mean a small motor launch. Uma
Samanta, the tehsildar has named it "Jalkanya." Uma is a poet
by temperament. The fellow who steers the boat is quite a babu.
His name Ramen, he chews zarda-spiked paan and wears a
wristwatch. It is inconceivable that he would ever get himself
in waist-deep water and wade like a pig in the mudbanks the
way Bishai does. When there's no passenger, he sits inside and
reads an old newspaper. Bishai leaves home at the crack of
dawn, and comes out here. The rest of the day and half the
night he spends at the boat landing. Once in a while his wife
comes down, shouts at him, and then goes back. That's all
she dares to do. Because once Bishai walks in the door of his
home, he will beat her up if she shouts. How many heroes are
there in the world who get drunk and do not beat their wives?
Bishai is drunk from the hour of sunrise, when he gives his pot
of rice-beer the day's first kiss, until after midnight, when he
comes home and drops on his back on the mat. Bishai's job is
just for the months from Asharh to Aswin. He has to keep the
boat clean, sweep and swab it, check the oil and petrol, and
push it close to the bank in any way he can so that the babus
can get in without difficulty. He does it until hemanta's chill
is in the wind, the sky turns a translucent blue, and walking
on the grass at dawn gets your feet drenched in dew up to the
ankles. That's when the river starts to wane. Then she stops all
this running and jumping and suddenly assumes a primipara's
shy quietness. Up in storage go the boats, the dinghies and
the Jalkanya. The contractor's agent then gets busy harnessing
the river. A jetty is made of three large boats placed next to
each other, held together with rocks and logs. On board go
people, cycles and scooters, even a jeep or a car depending on

the customer's status. Then ten or twelve strong labourers pull all three boats at once with ropes as thick as pythons. When that moving bridge crawls across like an enormous tortoise, sometimes Bishai too manages to find his way among the men smeared in mud and water. But that happens no more than six or seven days in a month; those labourers hate him. Why shouldn't they? How can a man with a helper's job for four months straight try to shamelessly beat someone else to the day's meal? Even so, if one of them is down with malarial fever or abdominal pain, Bishai is preferred to a chap from a different village, for he'll come running even for two rupees less.

After Magh, the river will grow thinner still, the sandbar wider. What now stays up like an open eye amidst briskly lapping water will then stretch bank to bank in the soft yellow sunshine, and the water will find its way through it in trickles. But, this swollen flow on its left, where I'm standing now, will remain much the same. The dark water's babbling won't cease, only those three crocodile rocks will stir up and rise out of the water. From Magh to Chaitra, people will be working to construct a fair-weather road. A narrow minimal road of earth and brick-dust laid on top of piled-up rocks and stones will go from this bank to that, paying the river scant respect. The sight of the river at that time will be saddening as if a beauty, who looked so gorgeous in Sravan, changed out of her luxurious Dhakai sari and put on a widow's plain Tusser!

Even when totally jobless, the hungry Bishai doesn't leave the ferry shed. So many from his neighbourhood move west, many others go north; the brick kilns there are in full swing after the rainy season. In those hard days so many families go away from the village—wife, children and all. In this place

the sky is then a brilliant blue, the winter chill bone-rattling,
the sun's warmth, once the mist clears, soft, nestling the body
as in a quilted shawl, the stubble of paddy plants in harvested
fields prickle the bare feet. Once the crop has been reaped,
threshed and sorted, work on daily wages peters out. Nothing
at all until Asarh; just sit and stare at the sky. Bishai never
could get himself to join the throngs of migrant labourers
going to other villages or a different part of the country. He
stays, holding on to the shed's porch—fearing that otherwise
even the four-month job may slip away! Bishai's wife feeds the
kids by slaving in people's homes and when that's gone, by
begging or whatever. Bishai sits by the liquor lean-to, waiting
like a dog by the butcher stand. His mud-smelling curly hair
tumbled over his forehead, his body bare except for the greasy-
filthy sarong around his loins, Bishai sits, his face on his knees,
dreaming perhaps of a future. In time, he could become
the launch driver; the work is no big deal, just sitting there
holding the steering, a bidi between fingers and hair groomed
with perfumed oil. And that Tukna, or Madna, whoever, he
could be the helper. Sitting in the cabin and just yelling 'Hey
Madna-Tukna' would be enough to get the bastard running,
sarong hitched up for action, saying 'Yes, huzur.' In his
drunken stupor Bishai doesn't even notice that behind the
shed, on the river's bend where the sun sets, the bridge is
slowly being transformed into a gigantic structure, as the ce-
ment-and-steel cage sheds the wooden posts and boards used
for pouring concrete. A sleeping dinosaur, as it were, slowly
standing up against the backdrop of blurred jungles. With the
forest land still not cleared and available, the approach road is
of course not ready yet. But, a climbing platform has been set
up with lengths of boards and strips of lumber. All those who
want to save the cost of ferry crossing and aren't carrying too

much, use that to climb up to the bridge and walk across. The road-department contractor crouches and waits, eyes shining like a wolf's, for the day the tender for road construction will be advertised in the newspaper. That's when his job starts, the stocking of raw materials begins. Another year at the most, or a year and a half. The bridge construction department will then remove the launch, boats, all this, and leave. Once the ferry service disappears, Bishai won't have his helper's job, even the skipper Ramen will have to pawn his wristwatch.

'Where is the ghat's light?'

I asked merely because I couldn't see Bishai anywhere close by. It's a constant problem, the bulb getting stolen. Yanus Kindo gives no answer. Yanus drives the tehsil jeep. He knows that if at this point he opens his mouth, the smell on his breath will fill the air. He has repeatedly been told not to drink during duty hours. Yet in just fifteen minutes when I stopped at the mission hospital at Kanakpur, the fellow must have taken a quick trip to the staff quarters at the back of the hospital. Jatin-babu does his best to keep an eye on him. But at that time Jatin was with me, carrying all the files. He wasn't near the car. Jatin is the one who now speaks, 'Please wait a little, let me look. Yanus, give me the matches.'

I know he has matches in his own pocket, but out of a quite unnecessary sense of respect for me, Jatin will never take the matchbox from his pocket. Yanus takes out a matchbox from the dashboard compartment and holds it out to him. In a blink of the matchstick igniting, everything surfaces before my eyes: the steep uneven broken path, the drizzle in darkness, the hissing black water. For just a fraction of a second and then all is dark again. Seeing me head towards the water, the rain over my head, Jatin cups his hands around his mouth and calls: 'Bi-sha-ai! Orre O Bi-shai!'

The answer comes as though from far away, swirling through a tunnel: 'Hawn, Agnyan! Anshi!'

In this darkness of night, a downpour imminent, he is standing somewhere in water upto his waist. Who knows what joy he derives from being in water! If there was any fish, he could of course use his gamchha to catch some. But where's the fish in the river these days? They say there was fish before the steel mill was built. Rui, katla, chital—big ones too. It's been thirty years now, the fish vanished from the day the poison disgorged by the mill mixed in the water. Thirty years! If only people could also vanish like the fish! Even after leaving the neighbourhood with their land taken over, so many of the families are caught in the mill's annual eclipse, living in torment like moths near a light. Getting land in nearby villages has not been easy. Where they did get it, they were unable to live off the rocky soil without water. Initially the mill took people like a crazed ghost. Overnight, a job contracting racket came up, and hundreds of non-local people got in with forged land papers. Most of the displaced are adivasis, they aren't as shrewd as the others. And even if they were, where's the money to pay a bribe? Some of the displaced farmers, getting jobs instead of land, went to live in the labour colonies. Gambling and alcohol have turned up at their doorstep. The babus who count the week's wages into their palms are also the owners of the hooch shop, they're the moneylenders, they're the gentry. Many, quite a few in fact, got neither land nor job. Without replacement land, the meagre fistful of compensation money they received was squandered away in drink and they came back, empty-handed again.

It's taken only one generation to open the eyes of the unemployed youth. The young man working at the furnace

as Mungru Oraon's son is, as everyone knows, actually Badri
Agarwal's nephew. He came from Rajasthan on a visit twenty
years ago; now he's permanently settled here. The landless
refugees have organized into morchas. Sit-ins, satyagraha,
periodic damage-causing incidents outside the factory gate, all
these things go on. Slogans written in red and black continue
to cover the town's walls; the blast furnaces confidently go on
spewing ash on the vegetation cover. After thirty years, the
descendents of the displaced are still running to the tehsil
office. The amin there, peering over his glasses, scolds them,
'What were your father and big brothers doing all this time,
sleeping tight, eh?' They're swarming everywhere you look—
genuine refugees, fake refugees. Those who're getting the jobs,
those who aren't! The fish escaped such prolonged agony.
Here they were, moving in shoals towards the sea, silver scales
agleam, and today they are no more. The chhokra inspector
who found traces of cyanide in the water, and was the first
one to report it, was sent away by the top bosses, transferred
right out of the district, much to the relief of the steel factory
managers.

   The boat comes to the landing, Bishai has brought it just
by pushing it. It's still about twenty yards from the bank.
Pushed any closer, its bottom will get stuck in the mud, then
it'll be hard to dislodge it.

   Meanwhile the rain has turned more energetic, the river
is unsteady. My small flashlight was right in my handbag,
but I didn't think of it all this time. Getting it out, holding
it in one hand, my sandals in the other, I step into the water.
Yanus has the files and papers all tied up in red shalu cloth
on his shoulder. There's another bundle in Jatin's hand. He
probably did not expect so much water. He looks both tense
and solemn. The water closes in on the ankles first, then the

knees, finally around the waist. Not cold, rather there's a kind of soft warmth about it. The embrace of the gently lapping waves is so entrancing that it seems as if it will put me in a swoon, and carry me off far beneath the water where the snakeworld lotus stays in bloom, lighting up the riverbed. But perhaps somewhere very near where my feet touch the sandy bottom, the ugly crocodile glides soundlessly in, opening its stony eyes with effort at the smell of a human. Ever since the day he found out I didn't know how to swim, Jatin has come to dread this ferry crossing. In a frightened sort of fashion, he follows me at a respectful distance, because even if he sees me going under, he'd be unable to rescue me because of the sheer embarrassment of touching me! He's a shy man. Out here, how would he find a suitably gray-haired old man or a policewoman if the need arose?

Suddenly, out of the water surfaces not a crocodile, but Bishai, pumping with both arms. His chest cage isn't that visible now, at least not at first glance, and his big eyes are flashing with a smile, his wet hair plastered on his forehead and neck. Very eagerly and very attentively, he's now lowering the platform board from the boat. He sticks a bamboo pole in the mud for me to hold on to, and insists on taking my sandals from me, simply won't listen to any objection. Ramen, who was in his dry dhoti and shirt all this time, sitting inside the cabin smoking his bidi—how can he keep away from this moment of greeting?—so, even he comes up, and pushing Bishai aside with a hidden shove of an elbow, leans out to me, saying, 'Ma, come, please come.'

Yanus will go back to his jeep. As soon as Jatin and I have got our shoes, umbrella, papers and so on in place and sat down, the engine is started and the boat sputters away. Bishai shines his jumbo flashlight over the water, revealing the rain falling on its light-smeared surface, the droplets mingling with the powdery light in the air. The big dark river keeps pulling us on farther—to the ghat under the tamarind tree. We move at a careful distance from the three submerged rocks, the moist wind blows on my cheeks and in my hair. My wet sari clings to me from the waist down to the feet, making quite a mermaid's tail; I feel mud between my toes and a chill through my body.

The motor boat goes around the sandbar, that wide-open albino eye, and crosses the stream on its other side. The water isn't that deep here, the waves soft and creamy. From the bank the wide path goes up gradually, it goes way beyond the tamarind tree and merges with the big road. Ah, here comes my own place, the so-called boundary of Mahuldiha. Sanatan is waiting under that tree, Kestopada too. And then finally the unbroken peace of the latticework verandah of the inspection bungalow and its garden. The watchman, awakened at this late hour, will run with the tiffin carrier to the roadside eatery and bring me some coarse-grained bran-red rice and tadka, or the ever-available lentil pakodas fried in cheap oil.

Crossing this river is something no one really wants to do. It means getting your shoes muddy, your clothes wet, it means catching influenza from being soaked to the skin. The officer sahebs try to sit right here in their Khamarpara offices and get their quota of meetings done for the record by asking the necessary people from the other bank to come over. Patients who are very ill come by boat to the hospital on this side to die. Of course there's a primary healthcare centre on that side too, but the doctor is away on vacation for eleven months in a year, looking after his thriving private practice in Swarupnagar. Before the monsoon deluge, the survey officials, the police, and other assorted servants of the people go back and forth on the fair-weather road briskly finishing their sleight-of-hand moneymaking—doing as many as ten inspections, reviews, investigations in a week. Stocks of medicines and supplies are sent to the hospital, the staff of the Khamarpara office quickly do the work of immunizing and distributing anemia pills by setting up a camp. And yes, in order to clear the road to promotion, the ambitious young doctors posted at the subdivision headquarters sterilize mothers by the hundred. Non-stop, between sunrise and sunset. Seeing it makes you a believer in the miracles of technology. If the boring of twenty tubewells can be done in a day, then why not two hundred surgical procedures, which require only human bodies to work on! In a dusty room of the panchayat office or high school, with tattered burlap curtains hanging outside, and people coming and going, no privacy at all, even stray dogs loitering with tongues lolling, some rat-gnawed cotton durrees are spread out on the cement floors. The call to order comes: 'Listen, will you? All the mothers here, let's have you quickly lie down. No telling if another visit can be arranged after the rainy season!'

It's near this very tamarind tree that Khamarpara block starts. Hansapal's crossing is a well-known address in this area. He has a petrol pump, a video library, an eatery, a motor-parts shop and a liquor shop. All the things needed for a highway. The tarred road to that crossing is shaded on both sides by great big arjun and gambhar trees. A few smallish office buildings, and a steamroller stand in front of the maintenance shed, getting old and preparing to die. No residential neighbourhood to speak of here. But there are a few hamlets edging the river to evade the grasp of Amdanga, Lautei, Kureshpur. Somehow the people in the villages

always get to know when I'm crossing the river. They come
to the tamarind tree and wait silently under it, with their
applications written on wornout paper or receipts carefully
tied into a corner of the dhoti or sari.

This bank has electric lights. Sanatan is near the car, I
don't notice him at first. He takes the bundle from Jatin's
hand. Bishai himself goes to the car, and deposits the pile of
papers he's been carrying on his shoulder. Poised to leave, he
ties the few rupees I give him in his waistfold and smiles his
heart wrenching smile and says, 'Ma, a job for me! The river's
here only two or three more months!'

'First, stop drinking, and don't raise your hand on your
wife…'

As with every other time, Bishai sticks out his tongue
and bites on it, swearing, 'Agnyan, I swear by the Goddess
Hangseswari, I never beat her!'

Jatin says under his breath, 'The chap'll run right now to
drink with that money.'

The swollen river in the dark, the boat, a cold Bishai
standing on the bank shivering—suddenly, I feel I must
extricate myself from all this and wake up to life.

Wiping the mud off my feet in the tender grass, I
become aware of feeling feverish, my whole body tired from
the unrelieved weariness of the last two days, my eyelids
growing heavy. Last night in Kusumdanga, the whole night
passed without electric power, in suffocating heat, with the
mosquitoes. The mosquitoes were so very energetic, all but
pulling the mosquito net off. At this moment, the memory
of the hot chapatis and pumpkin curried with singed dry
chillies, that I had at home in Mahuldiha before leaving on
this tour, is making me restless. All my senses are demanding
rest, a clean bed, even if it is without a pillow, and at least

five hours of unbroken sleep. It occurs to me that the time is now past ten o'clock; the cry of the crickets and the smell of wet leaf-grasses rising from the sleepy landscape around me remind me that it's night.

'Ma, come now. It is late.' Sanatan tells me.

'Please wait.' Someone approaches from under the tamarind tree. Do I know him?

A man not very tall, slender, in a khadi kurta, and dhoti. A folded white chador laid over one shoulder. I feel I've seen him somewhere. Jatin is tired, and a bit irritable. The tiredness is in his eyes, on his face.

'Can't this wait until after we get to the bungalow? This babu can go there!'

'I'm not going anywhere. What I've to say. I'll say here. We've been waiting for two hours. These people have got soaked in the rain. You must stop for a bit right here.'

Standing behind him are about thirty women, probably from Kureshpur. I know, because I can recognize the very old woman Tetri. Bent at the waist, toothless mouth, head shaved. Her home is in Kureshpur.

'Are you going to hold us up here?' Sanatan and Jatin-babu both turn around, spitting like wildcats.

This time I recognize him. How could I have missed the sound of the voice, the anglicized accent? It was in Delhi that I met him at a party at a friend's place. I'd heard that he was coming to these parts to work. Who would have guessed that he'd be waiting for me under this tree! Tousled black hair falling over the forehead, two huge eyes, bright behind his glasses, the young man smiles, and his smile lights up his three-day growth of facial hair. He too recognizes me; smiling he extends a friendly hand to me.

'Can you recognize me? I'm Stan D'Souza.'

'Oh, hello. I'm Kamalika.'

'I'm going to give you a little trouble. You can go after you've listened to us.'

'Why are you getting so defensive, Stan? Does it look to you as if I'm rushing, or are you in a rush yourself?' Right after I've said this, just as I feared—two cranes take off from the top branch of the tree at the sound of Stan's loud laughter.

'You haven't changed at all. But I'm not joking, we want to talk about last night's excise raid. It's urgent. You must have heard.'

Mentally glancing over the half-baked report I received around noontime, I said, 'I've heard. But I want to hear the details directly from all of you.'

Instead of waiting, Jatin has walked off to the inspection bungalow. He comes back with the watchman, who was heading this way with a piece of paper in his hand. In the low-wattage light, I read the paper. A message from my personal assistant Animesh despatched to the Khamarpara police station. Noticing the change of colour on my face, D'Souza asks with concern, 'Something bad, shall we talk later?'

'No, no, I don't want to leave anything for tomorrow.'

Lifting up her bent neck with difficulty, old Tetri says, 'Listen, Daughter, today we've come to really show you the marks on our backs.'

Trying with all my strength to swallow the hook of pain stuck in my throat, I say to them, 'Come, let's sit under this tree.'

2

The park is still there. Even though its face on the main road is blunted by the narrowing sidewalk, then twisted from the onslaught of a tuberail station. What was once the park's left sidewalk, covered with the krishnachura's red pollen, has long been taken over by hawkers selling rubber sandals, and after this the tube station also took a bite off the park's east corner. The meagre grass has disappeared because of continuous neglect and harsh treatment; the gravelly red dust is all that's left. Along the long narrow stretch of fenced ground edging its south side, where the gardeners Ananga and Batu once grew all kinds of flowers with water from a corporation tap, rows of shacks have come up, shacks roofed in old tiles and polythene sheets. Mantu's grandma no longer comes here, I'm sure she isn't alive any more. Nor that candy seller with one eye. The large group of elderly men—who would find empty benches close together each day and sit sadly through the yellow afternoons—has vanished. The small children, who toddled about looking for the conical kolkay flowers lying in the grass and, capping their fingers with those, pretended to scare each other as raksasas—they've all gone every which way with the play of night and day. Yet the park is here. For, until someone rubs it off the map of Calcutta, it has to go on living, its breath dwindling as it copes with neglect. For it does not belong to the special set of superordinates who were granted the blessing of death by wish.

The young wife, whose name was Chhabi, Chhabi-rani, used to come out here early, when the sun would still be sharp. Holding a small boy by the hand with his hair tied in a topknot, flat nose and smudged dot of kohl on his forehead. All mothers believe that the world conspires to cast an evil eye on their children. Chhabi-rani herself wasn't pretty. Her dark face was squarish, jawbones too high, hair tightly pulled back into a flat bun at the back. The cheap printed sari she wore, oddly pinned on her shoulder, somehow made her look like a hospital nurse. I often wondered why her sari stopped so much above her ankles, but never got round to asking her. One cloudy afternoon that Chhabi-rani put on an air of mystery—as if divulging a secret, and whispered to a girl of six: 'My husband, you know, he doesn't love me. He doesn't take me.'

Like an idiot the girl asked, 'Doesn't take you where?'

Paying no mind to the question, Chhabi-rani went on, her chin lowered to her chest, 'That's why my mother-in-law treats me so badly, my husband sees it, yet he doesn't care.'

No solution to her problem emerged from my head, and yet I felt as if my heart was being wrung. Getting up then, turning around and mouthing the players' chant, I ran off to join in a game of hopscotch with Gauri's group. The 'court' was drawn right on the footpath next to the vine-covered fence. When the markings faded from rain and the rubbing of shoes, it had to be redrawn with a piece of red brick. Two big safetypins were always attached to the bottom of Gauri's frock. Whenever we did not find a chip of clay or brick to toss, we played with one of her safetypins.

This hopscotch group consisted of Gauri, Minoti and Pori. Pori was fair, always looked fresh like a flower—she used to come wearing a green dacron frock, lighting up the park. A new outfit almost every day. It was at her initiative that we met at duskfall one day—each one of us was to tell of her sorrows. Minoti said her father often beat up her mother. Pori said, 'We've no sorrow, none at all.' Frowning, Gauri turned to me, 'Ei Babli, I bet you too have no sorrow?' Feeling troubled, I rubbed my back against the wall and said, 'But I have!' Gauri snapped back, 'Why, don't you and your folks get enough to eat?'

Solemnly I shook my head, 'No, not that kind of sorrow, but another kind.'

Gauri dismissed me blithely, saying, 'That other stuff isn't sorrow. If you don't get enough to eat, that's when you'll know what sorrow is.' I had seen her mother come out from the lane, in shabby widow's white, after doing shifts in this house or that. Some days Gauri would be with her, some days her sister Uma. Luckily Pori didn't know of this. If she knew, perhaps she wouldn't have let Gauri in to play. All the private goings-on in the neighbourhood could be seen from our window. Still, I was never able to accept Gauri's surpassing me like that when it came to the question of having sorrows.

One day, almost without realizing it, I became part of Mini's group's tag games. At one end of the park there was a white marble statue with an iron railing around it, a statue of that immortal dead youth holding his face up towards the tram lines. The plaque underneath read: "On the path of sunrise who do I hear say, Never fear, oh, never fear/For the one who makes a full gift of life, there's no wear, there's no wear." Looking up at his beautiful forehead, I felt my chest ache with anguish. Sometimes I'd gather some flowers,

champa and bokul, and leave them under the plaque. Even
though I had to squeeze in like a caterpillar through the gap
underneath, and out the same way. One day, coming out like
that, I caught sight of Mini's group at play. Somehow, this
game of tag struck me like bathing in the sea as the waves
come in. At first I couldn't see who was hiding where. Then
suddenly I saw Gopa's braided head near a bushy-top short
palm, and just when ten was getting close, Gopa shouted
'Ready' and, like a butterfly, darted off elsewhere. Then,
after a bit, I saw Mini cautiously creeping on her hands and
knees along the hedge of henna. If you aren't 'it', you've no
specific assignment and can dive into the game any time, as
I did. But Mini's group was forever looking for someone to
be 'it.' The smallish girl named Tulu in a shabby frock would
end up being 'it' over and over again. I could see that Mini
cheated while counting around the heads before each game.
Saying 'it' at the end counting aloud, Mini would give Tulu's
chest a push in a slightly cruel manner. Then the group
would scatter in search of hiding places. I used to hate Mini,
and fear her father. Still, for a long time I couldn't come out
of her group.

Mini's father used to sit on a bench guarding our sandals.
His blue lungi swayed over his ankle as one foot in a tyre
sandal rocked over another. Sitting there, the man used to
remote-control our games. He kept count of how many times
Mini was 'it', so she wouldn't be 'it' often. One day when I
went by him to pick up my sandals, he tweaked my cheek hard
and asked, 'Babli, how much salary does your father make?'
I felt quite insulted, as though my chappals with yawning
soles bore some intimate relationship with my father's salary.
I said, 'I don't know.'

'Find out and tell me tomorrow, okay?' he said.

I was afraid to ask my father, and so never let him knew what he wanted. One day I noticed that he wasn't going to guarding my sandals. With his foot he was pushing them away—as if they were defiled.

Another day close to duskfall I was about to run back home as the sky suddenly turned dark with clouds and I couldn't spot any of my playmates in their regular hideouts. Rain was already falling in large drops, and running to that broken-backed green bench, I found Mini's father gone, and no sandals there, not even mine. My new pair of rubber sandals, bright red like a bird's beak, with two cute holes on two sides! Bought just a few days ago, they had disappeared, flown away somewhere.

Mother said, 'Lose them one more time and you'll wear the torn sandals.'

This park held an odd kind of destructive fascination for me. At that time it was impossible to explain to anyone, only I was aware of it. A sort of spookiness about it drew me. Even on hot summer afternoons, I would come out here when it was barely three. Somehow I just couldn't stay home. At that hour even the rickshaw-pullers slept with their gamchhas over their eyes, and the door of the gardeners' shack was closed. The pathways around all empty, no one even by the fountain. Only a vagabond or two just like me, a madman or a beggar.

Why the park picked me out to cast its spells, I don't know. One day, a flying cricket ball shattered my glasses to pieces. I had neither the time, nor the wit to think of what might have happened had a shard got in the eye and, with the broken glass pieces folded in my frock, the broken frame in my hand, I ran home like one blinded. As I ran bawling out onto the big road, the houses, the buses, the trams, everything looked hazy as if covered in smoke. The Bihari who sold spicy digestive pills kept calling from behind, 'Hey khoki, what happened, where are you hurt, hey khoki!'

Wrapped in a page torn off an old math exercise book, I left the glass pieces, the frame, everything on the dining table. When he came back from the office, father, opened the packet and looked even before he'd hung up his sweat-soaked shirt, then said with a cheerless smile, 'Did you have to break them at the end of the month?'

Similarly, one night after dinner, as I got up to rinse my mouth and my mother was carrying plates and bowls to the kitchen tap; she suddenly stopped and looked at me, frowning. 'What's this! What did you do out there?'

My heart jumped. Was there something like soot on my cheek? Maybe a dead grasshopper in my hair that I hadn't noticed. My food-smeared hand froze in mid-rinse.

One of the gold rings I always wore in my ears was gone.

'No one took it, Ma, nobody touched my ear.' The tiny bit of gold must have fallen off while I was playing. I hadn't noticed.

In the darkness of the night the park was so still, it looked terrifying. Not a sound from those thousands of birds in the trees whose duskfall chatter was deafening. The lamp posts stood away from one another, each looking at its own foot, as if they had no duty to the surrounding darkness. With the help of flashlights, my father, I, and the youngest of my older brothers looked for the gold earring under bushes, in the grass and fallen leaves. So many things caught the light—cigarette foil, milk bottle caps, dislodged shiny buttons—whenever we saw anything shiny we crouched, searching carefully, but no trace of it anywhere! My brother said, 'Can you remember whether you had the earring on when you came by these keya bushes?' My father said, 'Babli, first try to remember the places you didn't go to this afternoon. Maybe then we can save some time.' Looking at that thick, world-obliterating darkness, I couldn't remember anything at all. The sun-filled yellow afternoon of the day seemed to have disappeared silently like a lone leaf from a saal tree's bare branches in winter. Tired from searching, we came home empty-handed when almost half the night was gone. Mother opened the door and, leaving it half-open, turned back in silence—she didn't ask anything, our sleep-deprived eyes and faces must have looked blank.

It's not the same with people. Those who get lost become fixed, framed in time. Their pictures out in newspapers, on television, keep them fixed for the rest of their lives. They don't grow older, their images don't change. If anything, they grow brighter in proportion to the time they're missing. But, by the same token, no one can know exactly what happened to them after they disappeared from the mouth of a lane. Kidnapper, sorcerer or a movie heroine's phantom smile on a hoarding—exactly who or what got stuck like a fishhook at the very base of their consciousness? Even among those who come back after getting lost, a kind of class difference is created. When back, one group is fussed over amidst family reunions. Another group, mostly small children and adolescents, meets with much beating and ill-treatment. The occasion of their return a reminder of the tension and inconvenience they caused by getting lost. What their parents remain most concerned about is if they're going to give them trouble by getting lost again. When I was very small, I got lost in this way for the first time from our house, which was the last house in the lane. I was four then. It was a winter morning. I was smeared with mustard oil, wearing only my oily knickers, right before getting a bath. Mother, who'd massaged my body with oil, had asked me to wait on the porch, and went in to fetch hot water, and in that short time I absentmindedly stepped outside. The honking of buses, the tangle of bikes, the great colourful hubbub at the end of the lane, all this drew me out as though with a long-handled hook. I walked a fair distance, unmindful of my bare feet. From what I heard later, I went past Benudi's tailoring shop, Lilabati Stores, the grocer's shop, the long blank wall of Raja's house, almost upto the crossroads where I started to get worried. Attacked by the fear of getting lost. The events thereafter were brief, of course. Just as my mother, leaving the hot water at the bathroom door, stood at the head of the lane, her throat hoarse from calling my name, Samir, a college youth from our neighbourhood spotted me running in tears and brought me back home. I was roundly slapped for this sudden misconduct and, outraged at this, I took revenge by rubbing my oil- smeared back on the whitewashed wall! The oil stain remained there for a long time. That was the reason I didn't tell anyone about my getting lost a second time. Nobody knows that even after straying a long way from home, I finally managed to return without getting really lost. Back home, I washed my feet at the tap and wiped residual dirt on the doormat, as on other days. Mother, who was adding the sugar drops from her evening prayer offering to the sugar jar, merely said, 'How come you're so late today?'

I'd noticed that man for quite some time, though. Thin, cadaverous looking, with thinning salt-and-pepper hair and a bald spot at the back, wearing a faded orange lungi and a dirty kurta, he would stand with a smile on his face at the place where we played among gym rings and parallel bars. He never went anywhere near the college youngsters or the older athlete types—as though he was happy just helping the kids reach up to the rings and down again.

The rings seemed very high in those days. Khokan-da the 'giantman' would go up the iron ladder and, with amazing ease, let go of one handgrip to catch the rod ahead, and continuing, reach the other end. I never managed to go beyond three bars. Just reaching for the fourth one felt as though the ladder was left far behind, and I was midstream in a river, unable to see either bank, my insides screaming to go back. Yet I had no way of making a turn and catching one of the bars behind. With a smile on his sunken cheeks the man would then quietly appear under the fourth bar, quickly grab me and lower me to the ground.

Khokan-da and his group used to hang out on the cemented terrace in front, at the very end of the football ground. Though I found it difficult to reconcile Khokan-da's bushy beard-moustache and hairy muscular legs with his short blue shorts, I never found anything lacking in his polite friendliness towards me. He never slighted me for being too little; on the contrary, he'd hold my hand, and pull me down to sit in their midst. Two or three times he even asked the one-eyed candy-seller over and bought me hot and lemony lozenges. Bantering as usual with his friends: 'The new girl Uttam has got in such-and-such film, know her name?' Bhaben, thin compared to him and clad in a shirt and trousers of the same colour would object: 'Hey, Khokan, watch what you say in front of a child!' Asim was the most dignified, handsome and gentle one in that group. With a soft smile he'd take my hand, saying: 'Come Babli, we'll take a little walk.' Walking by that wall covered in gulancha vines, I'd hear him humming—'With a flower garland, have me honoured'—a line from a Tagore song which he sang in a smooth flawless voice. As I walked, I'd dust the leaves with my hands, touch a flower briefly, or touch the large trees' bark and mutter something—at one point Asim looked at me smiling, and said, 'You love nature, don't you?' It took my brain several seconds to grasp that Asim's 'nature' meant the trees, the sun-smelling shrubs and bushes, the sky, all these, but his speaking the word 'love' made my whole body shiver. God knows, even back then a No. 8 notebook brimming with poetry lay hidden under my pillow—though, at the age of seven, the neighbours asked me endless questions about why I wasn't attending school, why I was still illiterate, and so on. To Asim's question, I could only nod shyly and say 'Yes, I do'. He patted my head affectionately and said—'In that case, Babli, you've nothing to worry about.'

But I was talking about that old man. One day, after a lot of rain, the park was filled with bright yellow sunshine the colour of a blackbird's beak. The madhavi vines gave off little showers every time the wind stirred their leaves. It rained so much that even the cemented terrace was wet in patches. Khokan-da's group was not sitting there that afternoon. The parallel bars were empty—as usual I was sitting on the ladder leading up to the rings. That old man came forward and held me and brought me down—then he started walking with my hand in his tight grip. I don't know why, but at the time I felt no urge at all to extricate my hand from his sweaty bony grasp— perhaps it was what's called hypnotism. He took me out through the park gate, across the road by the zebra crossing, past the zarda shop at the crossroads, the optics store, Sanguvelly restaurant, and far beyond. I don't recall how long I walked, only that we passed a cinema hall on the way. I was walking blindly; the man had not let go of my hand despite the many times I bumped against the moving crowd, through which he kept dragging me along, and despite my glasses repeatedly slipping down my nose from perspiration. I kept walking with my eyes cast down on the road, when suddenly something collided with my chest. A young shoeshine boy, running at top speed, pushed me aside and shot between us, as a wave of a crowd came running after him—and suddenly I discovered both my hands were free. At once I was overcome by a cold fear—and stumbling, I started running in the opposite direction. I ran across the zebra crossing not even looking at the traffic light, and got shouted at by the driver of a speeding taxi. Each moment I felt as though the old man's bony fingers were about to dig into my neck. Even when I was at the head of our lane, it was almost dark then, I didn't dare to pause and look back—a stray dog encouraged by my running, followed me down the lane, and quietly left when the front door was opened by my big brother.

This story of getting lost remained unmentioned home. But I had to tell Khokan-da and company—because I was frightened. I felt as though the old man's shadow was following me. Calmly, Khokan-da just said: 'I'll beat him up if he shows up again'. Asim told me the story of Sindbad and the old man. That old man, of course, never came back. But for a long time I wasn't free of a tendency to take fright every time I saw a faded orange lungi.

After this, I became detached from all groups, I'm not sure how. In the stillness of noon I'd come out here alone, walk around with a bare branch in my hand, read (without understanding) words written on the walls with chips of coal and brick. The park filled with people when the afternoon was well under way. People like Mantu's grandma, the group of old men, the lozenge-wallah, Chhabi-rani, and my occasional friends. With some I sat a little, stood around a little, but couldn't stay for long. As a result, finally, no group would let me in any more even if I wanted to play. They'd have me in only as an extra. Mithu-di openly told her groups not to include me. She was in the eighth grade, tall, fair, and had three groups of her own. Her verdict: 'Don't take her. Why does she switch groups so much?' I wasn't particularly unhappy about being alone. Except that Bishu's group of hoods started after me like four ragged wolves. Four boys of different sizes, all older than I, none going to school, always loafing about. Somehow they came to know that I was not attached to any group. Without warning, I'd be hit by a chip of brick or a large clod flying out of some bush or other. Or at duskfall on my way home, they'd follow me. One day I did turn on them in desperation when I was in front of the bus depot. I no longer remember what I said, but I exchanged blows with the gang. I alone, four of them. Bishu punched me in the nose, Monta snatched off my glasses and threw them away. Seeing my frock soaked in fresh blood, two bus conductors off duty came running up, and a few college students too. As the gang scattered and ran off, Benu-di brought some water from her shop's clay water pot and washed my nose and face. One of the bus conductors brought me the two lenses he picked up. The air there was heavy with the pungent smell of ground mustard from the oil mill. In wet frock and with broken glasses I went around the garbage dump and sneaked into my home like a thief.

This sorceress park dropped me suddenly one day, like a payloader's mechanical grip letting go. On a winter noon, Kutti-mashi was rolling with laughter chatting in the sun with my mother, and suddenly she glared at me and said, 'What are you listening to so hungrily? Come I'll enrol you in school. A big girl like you!' Despite my critics' dire predictions, I went to school, the way a paper boat floats, teetering down a rill.

But the school people must have been insane! They gave me
Tagore's *Sahaj Path* [the first primer] to read. At the time I had
been reading 'How much farther will you take me, O Beauty'
[Tagore's poem 'Sonar Toree']! Inside the green main gate,
the school for us kids was behind another small gate.

There were overgrown madhavi vines, a large field
with dust flying, the cemented platform-cum-stage. But at
first they wouldn't let me into the large red building. The
class for us youngsters was held in the saline-stained small
building. At the mouth of the passage to the small building
there was an unused old cement tank which supposedly had
ghosts dwelling in it. One day, fearful of going there alone,
I darted across the tank screaming 'Baba re, Ma re,' when
a great big slap landed on my cheek. 'Are you blind? Can't
you see people?' Gita-didimoni, the teacher, stood before me,
glaring like a blast furnace through her bottle-thick glasses.
Ruma-didimoni, pretty in her gold bangles and bell-flower
earrings, a red-yellow butterfly in her printed sari, passed by
saying, 'Aha, Didi, she really has bad eyes, poor thing!' In the
initial days, I often thought of running away from school.
Coming out on the pretext of having a drink of water, I'd
hold my hand under the running tap for a long time and
watch the water flow through the hairy tendrils of soft moss
in the drain below. Coming out to sharpen a pencil, I'd watch
the deep blue sky, the white cloud structures forming, and not
feel like going back in at all. One darkly clouded afternoon,
after hearing an announcement that the geography class was
cancelled, we were all jumping up and down on our benches
and jostling about. Just then, the drawing teacher Dipti-
didimoni, who had a twisted leg, limped her way up, sat down
at the table, wiped the sweat off her forehead with a white
handkerchief and said, 'Come, let me show you some colour

tricks.' Then, on a white sheet of paper slowly appeared a clump of bamboo, a dark shade under it, a hazy marsh, a befuddled yellow frog. She drew in the stripes on the frog's back, put in its bulging eyes and finally added some broad leaves, and said to us, 'You see, how the magic goes.' It was pouring outside and in the half-light inside, we were elbowing each other to lean over the table to watch her drawing.

In this manner, Babli merged with a passel of uniform-clad schoolgirls. As long as I wore dresses made of assorted printed fabric, I had a face of my own, a face different from any other. After losing that, what I found was a sun-scorched stretch of sickly sidewalk—with piles of shit at places, melting tar spilled off a tar barrel somewhere else, a hand-drawn hopscotch court somewhere, a garbage bin overflowing somewhere else. In front of the cobblers' shacks, their wives had hung just-washed clothes on the clothesline—wet dhotis, colourful saris flapping in the wind and smelling faintly of washing soap and soda! This was the route we followed daily to school.

Beyond the zebra crossing, if you step past the begging bowls laid out on the steps of the Radha-Krishna temple and walk on some distance, taking the turn near the house with the green porch, the deep blue sky comes into view on winter days, above the thick growth of trees at the end of the road. The time of year when the smell of orange peel stays on the fingers. From the by-lane where they play cricket rises a shout everytime someone is out; and suddenly, at that sound, an entire flock of pigeons takes flight. Perhaps the annual exams have just finished or perhaps they're still going on, and the top knuckle of the middle finger is stained dark from all that writing, while the mind lingers on the thought of the impending vacation—a boundless vacation after somehow getting that blue report card home.

When the rains come, this route will once again be totally transformed. How on earth can so much water collect in just a couple of hours of rain? How can so much filthy, disgusting stuff flow out on to the flooded streets? Why is it that wet shoes will not get dry, even when kept under the fan? The fans at school were the old-style ones on DC current, they produced more noise and sparks than air flow. We'd have to sit all day in wet clothes, and wet shoes, and my feet would hurt in the evenings after coming home, my skin would itch from walking through dirty water. Once, in my thirteenth year, when wading through the rain-logged street, I suddenly felt a kind of private thrill of freedom. Rainwater spilling over the umbrella soaked me to the skin—but there was no one around to hurl catcalls. All those pre-monsoon heroes who'd be hanging out at street corners with their hands in their pockets and shirt collars raised—they were all gone. Looking far, far through my steamed-up glasses I'd take in the landscape—sleeping rickshaws, pushcarts with handlebars up in the air just standing still and getting wet, in a river of murky water undulating to the horizon, no sign of people even in the surrounding homes, only a few kids from the city corporation school sending pebbles skim-hopping across the water…. The street bandits all driven off by the monsoon's full blast. How they had harassed me in spring and the pre-rain summer! I'd walk the streets with eyes fixed on the sidewalk, making no eye contact, and despite this, on the day exam results were to be declared, someone would stand in front of me, arms outspread blocking the way and demand: 'Ei, aren't you going to give us sweets?' Laughing, another would step forward and draw him away, saying, 'Stop it, why bother the good girl?' All of it planned, staged. Before the neighbourhood barware puja they'd come up to me and say, shaking the yellow or pink

billbook at me, 'No passage without a subscription.' After
about the third time I looked up and said, the words just
tumbling out of my mouth: 'I don't have money with me and
even if I did, I wouldn't give it to you.' After that they stopped
asking me for a subscription. Then, there was the unemployed
Manik Datta, a self-styled wellwisher, sort of a live-in uncle.
He mistook my friend Tuku's boyfriend for mine and having
kept his suspicions to himself for a long time, followed me
noiselessly upto Hariram's laundry one day, then shouted at
me suddenly, 'The truth now, who's he to you?' Tuku had
briefed me early on that if anyone ever asked me this, I was to
say he was her elder sister's sister-in-law's younger brother-in-
law. After hearing me say that, Manik Datta left discouraged,
not knowing how very tired I was from drafting her replies to
two love letters a week. Tuku felt insulted when I complained
once, 'You say he's studying for the B.Com., then why does he
misspell so much?' She snapped, 'What's the point in finding
his errors, why don't you just write what I'm telling you?'

   I don't know why Manik Datta did not hang out on the
street corner when it rained. Could it be that just standing
there holding an umbrella over his head would look a bit
strange? Sometimes I'd see him in a pair of gumboots walking
towards the marketplace. Perhaps that was because his elder
brothers' wives made it hard for him to stay home on rainy
days, unemployed as he was.

   Why did I have to write so many love letters for others?
After one or two letters of mine became hits with Kushal
(Tuku's boyfriend), Shabari came to me too, and so did Mita.
They'd keep talking and I'd compose the letters by arranging
and rearranging their words. Mita had such a sharp tongue,
I didn't go near her if I could help it. Once, only once, I had
opened my mouth to her: 'How come you're not in uniform

at school? At once she hissed at me, 'What can I do, we aren't rich like you, the only school dress I have got wet yesterday, it still isn't dry, should I then—'

I ran from the spot with my hands over my ears. Mita's father did not live with them; her mother and the four siblings lived in one room in a slum. Once in a while when the father came, they drove him away by throwing brickbats and shouting abuses at him. Mita too had a boyfriend, of whom she said, 'He says he goes to college, who knows if he's lying or telling the truth.' Even such a naagini-like Mita once turned sadly to me, 'Look, he's written that he wants to kiss, maybe he thinks of me as a bad sort. Now, come on Babli, write a stern reply for me.'

These days, this side of the city is almost covered with jatra advertisement posters carrying a drawing of a grown Mita's face. Such a complexion, and such a beautiful figure she has even at age thirty-five! Her photographs appear quite often in various weeklies. Whenever I see her image now, I am suddenly reminded of her two big toes peeping out of the torn keds on her feet.

Well, what am I doing here standing at this four-lane crossing? It's Saturday today. I'll take the night train back. Now I've to go straight, towards Sealdah. Or should I first go to College Street, where I haven't been in a long time, to spend this bit of time that I have, snatched from work and colleagues? When Guddu or Kuki are not with me, I like to indulge in a little aimless wandering. Along the way, all of a sudden, I have paused by the park. That rakshasi from long ago, very old and doddering, now, has caught me in her invisible grasp and watched my inner thrashings gleefully. Sometimes, when I sneak out here, I search for that little girl—who once, watching the flood of red that came with the sunset, wished to break the window bars and fly off. The bars didn't bend even a fraction, only night descended before her unblinking eyes, a star-studded night. In her dreams she has flown in that sky so many times on two immense white wings, looking at the sleeping tramlines and the winding roads flowing like waterless riverbeds. Then, tired from flying among deserted moonlit rooftops, she has at one point paused near her own house and watched: there is no one there, the house empty as if no one had ever lived there. How unbearable it felt in the dream, this shock, this firm rejection from the closed-up house, this solitariness!

Why did the power of her glasses suddenly jump from minus three to six? She had done nothing to abuse her eyes; instead, each morning she had splashed cold water on her eyes as if it were a religious rite, sat with her palms over them for two-and-a-half to three minutes, though she continued to read books from dawn to dusk and, in the afternoon, or at supper—until someone would slap her on the back out of concern and would snatch the book away.

'Won't I be able to read story books any more?' The elderly doctor Mahimaranjan Ray had frowned first, screwing up his puffy eyes and then smiled like a compassionate deity in response to her question. He must be tired from all that work of bringing light to the blind. "Why, daughter, you'll read everything, how will you grow up otherwise, just make sure there's enough light in the room—" Back in her room with the joy of someone just spared the gallows, she picked up Anton Chekhov, but no sooner had she done that, there was an angry voice from behind—'Put it down, put it down.'

'The doctor said it's all right if there's enough light in the room.' With this reply she ran to a corner of the room to be by herself. I know it's impossible to find that girl now. Her outgrown canvas keds, her worn belt, her absurd tunic, her faded saris with frayed borders—the objects that marked the history of her journey in the period following her escape from the grip of this old sorceress—they're all scattered here and there. Pebbles along the riverbank, the river gone. Of the child, the adolescent, who gradually grow up, where does the childhood state get left behind?' This ceaseless evolution, the shedding of the bark of time along the way—is it that different from death, any less grievous? Just as a human being vanishes at death, and doesn't return even if you're hungry to see him one more time, and only the insignificant remains of life stay on, so it is with one's vanished childhoods.

There were those through whom I have evolved, through whom this 'me' has taken birth—the utterly spellbound, naive adolescent in a knee-length frock, her spectacles sliding down to her nose, hair wet and done up in two tight braids; the young girl of eighteen running for a No. 2B bus, stumbling after it, her not-yet-accustomed feet getting caught in her sari, on her still immature arms a delicate network of veins visible in the morning sun—these vivid images…does the immersion, the letting go, of these images amount to anything less than death? I'm here, in all my elements and my senses. I'm here, yet they are gone, and no magic can make them come back in the midst of this laughter and play. Just as the newborn Guddu will not return, that waxdoll in a tiny singlet with closed fists, his dreamy smiles in sleep, his surprised turning of head as he hears a bird sing in noontime quietness and then gazing at the endless blue.

A tram turns the crossing on the big road and is approaching. Is it a No. 24 or a No. 27? Depending on that, it will go from here to Dharmatala via Khidirpur or along the Diamond Harbour Road directly to the Behala tram depot. At this moment I've no need for a tram. Old, pathetic like a circus animal, it approaches with a clanking noise, its body plastered with blue ads for small savings. A long time ago, when at night's end the streets used to be hosed down with Ganges water from the hydrants, and a whole clan of pigeons would noiselessly descend from all the bay windows to eat the peas and lentils scattered by Bhanu the grocer, then this metallic sound of a tram turning a bend used to rise over the maze of tracks and, barely awake, I'd see a bloodless moon setting. The memory of my interrupted dreams was mixed with that metallic sound.

The city had not yet become so tired, so ugly, age-worn. When the tube rail came up these days of the trams' sprint along the edge of the Esplanade's green, conversing with the line of eager trees, were over. Now they make a lot of detours, pass by a great many crowds, edge a lot of indifference and ugly walls. With that weariness of aging in its body, the tram somehow drags itself on and passes by.

3

Laughing, and knowing he won't get an ashtray, Ajayendra puts out his cigarette on the cement ledge of the windowsill. He pitches the stub on the grass outside and says in mock jest, 'I'm going to be finished.'

'You know that I won't sign any report that gives Rupak Misra a clean chit.'

'I'll be finished.'

'Then let there be two reports. You write yours and I write mine.'

'Two contradictory reports? What do you think they will say?'

'How does it matter what they say, Ajay?'

Ajayendra glances sharply at my face. A smile darts through his eyes. Then he says: 'You're quite ruthless, you know. I told you right at the beginning how much trouble I had gone to come here. And why I've spent a lot of money, to get the children admitted in a residential school, and I've come here to stay out of trouble for at least three years. Madam, this stint is absolutely crucial for me! If I get transferred, I'll have to tell Shyama who's to blame. She'll come and do battle with you. Agreed? Don't tell me you aren't afraid of Shyama?'

I was watching Ajayendra closely. Police Superintendent Ajayendra, about four years younger than me. Married very early, he's already a father of three. About five feet ten inches in height, with a bright dark-skinned polished appearance, his silk-brown hair trimmed close to the head, tinted glasses on his eyes, and a serious-looking hefty moustache. He's wearing a light pink sports shirt, sparkling white trousers, and brown shoes polished enough to make a fly slip. Regardless of whether Ajayendra happens to be in a coalmine or in a flood-ravaged village, a mild masculine perfume emanates from his body. When he has to spend twelve hours on the road, he must change his clothes at least once; and he never sets off on the road without an icebox of cold drinks. Next to Ajayendra I look untidy and dishevelled, at the evening district-level get-togethers, and on the road. Hardly ever using a comb when on the road, with mud on my feet and on my sari's lower edge, in the same predictable plait wherever I go, the same pair of white-stone earrings, a bangle on the right wrist, a watch on the left, that's all. When I return from a tour, a layer of the road's red dust covers my hair. Staying neat like a butterfly, as they say, is perhaps unattainable in this birth for me.

Ajayendra's wife Shyama is much younger than him and is very expressive when she talks, using her hands, face and eyes. A girl from Arrah district, she's fair, small and already her young age has at least ten kilos of excess weight. Her body is covered with gold jewellery. She has sometimes visited my home in Mahuldiha. Frowning, she'd insist like a child, 'My goodness, Didi, how can you stay like this! Come, let me make you over! Bring out a good sari.' Yes, I do fear Shyama, especially when she starts pulling me by the hand to do what she wants. Stubborn girl. Ajayendra too fears his wife. The things he has just told me are not his own thoughts. They are Shyama's thoughts but his words. This is a subject of light banter between me and Ajayendra—not meant for the public.

In a short while Ajayendra and I look at each other smiling.

Lifting his hands over his head, he stretches and says, 'Uff, when *fallen under the yavans' rule, you must dine together on forbidden food*—go ahead and call Girin, give him your dictation, let the joint report be done with, whatever the fates may hold for me.'

'Wait, wait, you sound as if I'm imposing my opinions on you. I didn't talk to the women by myself, you were there too—are you forgetting that?'

'Um-m,' his gaze brushes his hands; he's slightly bored, and annoyed, 'I don't believe that story about torn blouses. Those bastard reporters, we shouldn't have let them get there before us. I told you so the day before yesterday—then the newspaper stories wouldn't have come out before our statement.'

'I can understand your not believing that story. But your idea of stopping the reporters was crazy. Only two of them went in their own cars, the other five in private taxis—the union had arranged to bring the reporters from Kumardihi. Should we have highjacked them on the road, or called a press conference and lured them into a hotel? And would they have come even if we'd done that? According to information from at least five sources, Misra drank excessively before going on the raid. Didn't he?'

'That he did.'

'There wasn't even a reliable intelligence report with Misra that there'd be sabotage during the strike. The company had made no written request to him to the effect that labourers from the minority union were afraid to come to work; if the company had done that, you would have known about it before the others. Now I hear a warrant was pending against Ignes, none of us knew about it, it was activated only the day before the strike. The police force went there and flung away the slum people's pots and pans, their mats and clothes. They didn't spare even their chickens, they took them away. They had some management supervisors and brokers with them, who identified the huts and also took part in dragging the women out, even a pregnant girl who had come to her mother to have her baby…'

'Many of them do illicit liquor brewing, don't you know that?'

'All I know is that generations' of them have traditionally brewed their own mahua and rice liquor, but now Suresh Bhatia's agents have opened liquor shacks in all the slums. By what means can they put food in their stomachs that you wouldn't consider a vice, Ajay?'

'They always thrust the women in front, they know you'll become emotional. Please don't mind, but if you were a man, they wouldn't have portrayed the incident in such dramatic terms. Never mind, come, let's get the report written.'

Girin, my steno, comes in with his notebook. He has come with me from Mahuldiha, with typewriter, paper, carbon, the works, their availability here being uncertain. This inaccessible range of hills laden with iron ore is at least two hundred miles west of Mahuldiha, past Kumardihi, bypassing Lorka, edging on the district's south-west boundary. Ajayendra and I have come at the same time for the investigation; this sort of coming together doesn't happen often these days unless it's an emergency case. We both keep busy, with our respective spheres of duty. My hands are quite full with the drinking water problem, the yield of paddy, the irrigation schemes, family planning, schools and colleges, the land revenue system. Ajayendra too has his responsibilities: law-and-order, inspection, and added on now, the different duties of staff housing. This small hilltop colony is located in a place called Chiri. There must have been a village with that name here at some time. Now that the iron mine is quite established, the place has acquired an urban look, with the building of staff quarters, a club house, and a guesthouse, surrounded by scattered slums where coolies and labourers live. People from ten or twelve nearby villages also come to work here, they take various shortcuts through hillside pathways. Those who lived some distance away, have built shacks, and huts roofed with tin or tiles, and settled down here. Most of them do contract labour—various contracting agencies recruit them for casual work, and lay them off on all kinds of excuses. They defer paying the wages, spend nothing on account of medical treatment, flicking off disabled workers like flies and pitching them into a pit of foodless days. There's a small dispensary at Chiri, a twenty-bed general hospital too, but only for the company's staff and regular workers. Last year, Ignes and his group had to spend one whole day running from one place to another, carrying three labourers who'd been injured in a truck accident—the government health centre said the case didn't belong to the area it covered, the doctor at the dispensary in Chiri said the case was in its jurisdiction but the labourers were hired not by the company but by the contractor. Two of the injured died of excessive bleeding, one ended up disabled and laid off. And we have such high moral standards that if their wives and daughters brew liquor, we don't hesitate to categorize them as women deserving rape!

Ignes, the local leader of larger union, once took me to a meeting of their night school. Seven or eight very young men and women, and a middle-aged mother of four who have quietly been tutoring illiterate labourers over the last four or five years, even running a playroom for their small children. They receive no grant money and work with used books, cracked slates, scrounged-up blackboard and duster, chalk bought from subscriptions, a few sooty hurricane lanterns, or a bulb hanging from a stolen connection. After I had made the Chiri dispensary take in the emergency cases and filed a complaint against the doctor, I could sense that Ignes exempted me from his distrust. Could I do something for their students? I sat down a while watching them perform a play they had written, then the youths invited me to visit the slums of Zones three and four. It was in number three that Ignes, standing before an almost collapsed shack, scolded an old woman, 'So Mashi, here's a guest, offer her a few sugar drops at least and a glass of water!'

'No, no, there's no need for that!' I meant it, I didn't have the time either.

Putting a sugar drop in my mouth, I absently took the glass without looking at it. I was about to touch it to my lips, when a muffled roll of laughter rose from the gathered crowd. I looked then. 'What's this, what have you given me to drink?' Muddy, foul-smelling, reddish brown in colour—was this water?

Looking directly at my face, Ignes said, 'It is water. Hakim-saheb, this is the water we drink. People like me boil it and strain it—and this old woman, Mangru's grandma, she fills her bucket from the nullah and drinks it straight, they don't have either the wood or the kerosene to boil it.'

'You drink water from this nullah? And the piped water in Chiri—'

'That's for the company folks. We're only the contractor's labourers.'

They were all smiling snidely. Some of the young girls with arms around each other's waists, covering their mouths with fists full of saris.

'No tubewell installed here?' My ears were hot from the humiliation.

Ignes solemnly replied, 'Three or four borings were made, none of them worked. No water came up. There is a problem because of the rocks. But we're working on an alternative estimate, look at this—Jewel, bring the drawing.'

They were quite prepared. It was an evening covered in winter mist, a layer of smoke in the air over the slum, in the distance the sodium lights atop the hill. The old woman was holding up a kerosene lamp; Jewel and a young girl were explaining to me from a hand drawing they had unrolled. It was on cheap paper, in poor-quality ink; but, very carefully drawn were the course of the nullah, the geometry of the pipelines, the manner in which the pipes could be extended so that eight slums would get water from the first phase. This many thousand feet of pipe, priced at this rate, this many thousand rupees in total cost. The calculations were promptly carried out orally.

'Where are you going to get so much money from? The company isn't going to pay for this.'

'Why do you think we asked you over, Madam? We're putting this water in a bottle, take it with you, whenever you're thirsty remember us. And perhaps the memory will bring forth an idea, why not wait for it to happen? Where's the rush? After all, independence is only forty-five years old!'

They would not relent, they saw to it that a bottle of the water was sent back with me. The design too: 'Take it. We have a copy.'

That bottle stands on my dining table. Once, when Guddu was visiting Mahuldiha on vacation, he asked, 'Is this alcohol?'

'No, it's water.'

'I know, it's water for the poor, isn't it Ma?'

'How did you know?'

'When I was little, you once beat me for drinking this kind of water.'

Guddu had once happily drunk cupped palmfuls of the muddy water that comes crashing down in the rainy season from the forest nullahs in Dishergarh. It was immediately followed by a beating, from me. Luckily for me, Guddu went back to the pages of his book and did not prolong the discussion, or the change of colour on my face wouldn't have escaped his notice, even though he was so young at the time.

This place called Chiri is very beautiful. My friends in Calcutta say, 'You must have been to Chiri, since you are posted in Mahuldiha. Fan-tas-tic!' The tar-paved road goes winding up the hill, at the most enchanting point of which stands the company's guest house, a three-storeyed building. The air-conditioned rooms of the top floor on the right are authorized to be opened when VIPs visit. Arriving here in darkness of the night one can hear the wind's soft breathing, and the strumming of crickets. One can see the lights in the distance like isolated clusters of fireflies and yes, even in the hot season on the Chiri hill the breeze is a cool hand on one's cheek—during winter the temperature here sometimes touches zero. At night it is impossible to even imagine the supremely beautiful treasures here that the darkness hides under its wings spanning air and sky! Below these steep hills are forests of saal and teak, tens of thousands of trees, their green leaves vibrating like a million dragonfly wings, their vibrant presence along the slopes of the hills, nourished over thousands of years through the caressing sun and rain and wind, transforming them from seeds to saplings to young trees. When the sun rises in this forest, that sunrise is the stuff of poetry. It rises everywhere, and spreads throughout the woods, falling on every streak of rock, the face of the earth glowing as light touches its surface. If you haven't seen this sunrise you have seen nothing in Chiri. I've seen this sunrise. But I don't know whether to call it misfortune or good fortune that Ignes and his friends did not let me get away with my senses steeped in its pure pleasure. On various pretexts they kept holding before my eyes the underside of the sunrise, as of the exquisitely embroidered nakshi-kantha...

'It's very cold, Madam. Mangru's grandma, poor old woman, she'll probably die this time. Why don't you use the heater, there's the plug point in that corner!' ...Or, 'Have you looked at our plan drawing? Has anything come up concerning the water?'

Ignes in his old corduroy pants, stained with grime and soot, a blue jacket and an ancient pair of canvas shoes, Ignes with his sun-scorched coppery skin, kept popping up before me everywhere like an evil spirit. A long horizontal line on his forehead with brows raised, the hair short and kinky, Ignes remains stuck at the back of my middle-class conscience, like a shadow or maybe like a leech. When released from police custody this time, Ignes will no longer be forgiving towards me. Or maybe he will. Because in the meantime he has perhaps figured out that I am no walking embodiment of humanity, I am a front pincer of this entire system. Since I'm by nature a sturdy sort, some simple souls mistake me for an autonomous entity apart from the rest.

On the pretext of arresting Ignes, Rupak Misra and his gang turned up well past midnight, upto their gills in alcohol. The management came along, and so did the contractor's agent. Turning the homes upside down, tossing and scattering their belongings, they proceeded to rape the women in self-assured confidence—knowing that no one would bother to travel two hundred miles of hills and forests to read their petitions written with unpractised hands on grubby paper. Luckily the young men, banding together, stopped them. They too had sticks in their hands. What was written in the F.I.R. about knives, axes, and explosives was done under direction from others more powerful than them. Many were charged for armed attack, assault and the crime of obstructing government forces on duty. Ignes was not found there that night. Perhaps he had taken off beforehand, smelling the raid. He was arrested in this afternoon, a day later. By then the strike was limping along here and there, like a spider with its back broken. But the coming of journalists was one thing Ignes and his associates managed to arrange quite fast. They took care of the cost of transportation in bringing them to this no-man's-land. As a matter of fact, even Ajayendra and I learnt about it from the newspaper. By that time there was a mild uproar in the capital, press clippings of photographs of tribal women in torn blouses had reached the legislative assembly and started disrupting things like firecrackers. I was getting phone calls one after another. 'Kamalika, what are you doing! Go there, do a joint investigation.'

'How could this happen?' One of the bosses demanded.

'The whole thing is very unfortunate, the area is inaccessible, this sort of atrocity perpetrated on slum people under the cover of night's darkness—!'

'Ah, who's asking about atrocities, couldn't you have stopped these reports?'

'How?'

'Anyhow. You could've called a parallel press conference, in some good hotel at Kumardihi. How could they get there before you?'

Indeed, we were very slow in responding. No, not because we couldn't strangle the media or mount a forceful counter-campaign, but because we lost their trust. Now, after all this, if I go there and stand at someone's door, will I be given muddy water with sugar drops even if I ask?

The joint report is done at last, Girin has typed it well, more or less error-free. It has been sent on the wireless, and a courier is also taking it to the capital by the night bus. Perhaps those who are responsible for the incident will get punished, the management too might make some restitution under pressure from us. This time perhaps a small bit of money from the tubewell fund will get thrown at them like mudi-mudki. New thatch for some of the huts, blankets, milk powder, some petticoats and blouses for the young women, and there'll be speeches too. Assurances from the elected politician. A medical team will come to give the women a checkup, distribute free iron tablets and colourful cheap vitamins wrapped in paper. Jewel, the one who had so enthusiastically shown me their design for drinking-water supply by the light of an oil lamp one winter evening, now watches me silently, one hand on the fence post, the other in his pocket. He hasn't come near me, hasn't asked for explanation; I would've felt better if he had, I could then have explained a few things to him. It's better this way, that he hasn't wanted to know anything. Otherwise, I would have to lie again. I'd have to say: Don't misunderstand me, I and those men who came here two nights ago are different. I'm with you, they're on the opposite side.

Lalmati's mother who had brought her pregnant daughter from Badabuli to be with her for her first delivery, was crying as she talked to me. 'I brought her over from her in-laws' place, talking them into it with such sure pride, but then I couldn't protect her.' To her daughter she said, 'Show her, show this Didi where you've been hurt.'

Lalmoti, barely past adolescence, with a swollen belly, the end of her mill cotton sari covering her breasts, her feet and fingers quite puffy, held her breath for a few moments, fixing her gaze on me, hate and fear in her dilated innocent eyes. Then she shook off her mother's hand, clutched firmly at the blouse over her left breast where the scratchmarks were and said: 'No'.

The narrow road edging the foot of the hill is still wet from the rain. It goes winding up, the rise of hills on the right, the drop of ravines on the left, and the forest-covered valley in between. Descending from the hill, this road slopes gently and merges with the state highway forty kilometres west. The two cars move quietly in the dark, the red light atop Ajayendra's car turned off. He's sitting on my right, by the window. We'll get back to Mahuldiha tonight, via Kumardihi, no matter how late it gets. We started out day before yesterday. Both of us are tired. After getting back in the car, neither has spoken to the other. For quite some time Ajayendra fidgets in his seat, a slight tension at work inside him.

Quietly I say to him, 'If you want to smoke, go ahead. I don't mind.'

'Oh, many thanks.' Instantly his hand goes to his pocket. He holds the cigarette away, his right hand extending outside a bit. He reacts to my kindness by acting like a camel allowed inside a tent in the desert! Intelligent young man. Again, silence for a while.

Clearing his throat he says, 'I beg your pardon for making that remark.'

'Which one?'

'I said, they push the women ahead when they see you; that was a rotten thing to say, terribly unfair, please do forgive me.'

'Are you still feeling guilty on account of Misra?'

'How did you know?' Even in the dark Ajayendra glances at me, smiling silently. 'A bit, yes,' he says. Quite a smart, competent young man. He's had quick promotions too. This could prove to be a blot on his career. I know his family; we were neighbours for some time in Jabalpur when I was young. That's why I'm feeling a little upset. He adds: 'I'm the villain, after all. No name from your section came up in the report! But I had to mention Rupak's name. My subordinates will never be able to forget this.'

Annoyance edging my voice, I say, 'Ajay, in all this time I haven't been able to make you understand one thing. You still haven't shed this habit of thinking who's under me and who's under you. Are we any different? Depending on the circumstances, the names that come up in the reports belong sometimes to one section and sometimes to another. Most times no names come up at all. No one even gets to know what's going on in the darkness of night, or even in broad daylight. Perhaps I haven't told you about this: that day when I was crossing the river on my way back from Jarangloi, Stan was waiting for me at the Khamarpara ghat, with old Tetri and some of the young wives and daughters from Kureshpur. The first time I went to Kureshpur, they were glad to see me. "Great!" they said, "We can now show you the marks on our backs, we won't have to cover ourselves up to enter your office". I didn't even imagine that so soon after that there'd be marks on their bodies again. Your men were not involved in that raid. My excise forces were. But, in effect, what is the difference?'

'You haven't told me about this.'

'There was not much to tell, Ajay. We haven't left any scope for the histories of Kureshpur and Chiri to turn out any different. There's just one difference, the adivasis there are all small or landless farmers; unlike Chiri no iron ore has come out of the ground. Old Tetri was telling me that when she was young, men and women both drank rice liquor on festive occasions, mahua liquor was available at home all year round. But beating one's wife, thrashing one's children—all that has started recently. Khamarpara now has two licensed country liquor shops, yet in every village liquor is brewed for sale—the agents of Suresh Bhatia, Johnny Agarwala and the like have this whole area under their thumb. Drinking and gambling. The stupid men pawn wristwatches, transistor radios, bicycles, everything they have, then come home and make trouble. I was the one who suggested to the women, "Why don't you get together and give the men a good thrashing once in a while?"

'They looked at me with doubtful eyes—"But that's forbidden in the shastras, you know, the raising of your hands against your men." How can it be, I asked them. In that case, raising hands on women must also be forbidden in the shastras.

I went out of my way to tell them the story of Sitamma of Nellore. How the women in Nellore organized themselves to picket the liquor shops after reading about Sitamma's anti-liquor compaign in their literacy centre. They listened and their eyes shone with interest. And after I had made them listen to that account, the excise forces under me went on a raid, ostensibly on my orders. They broke some ten or twelve liquor vats in homes, dragged the women out, ransacked their belongings and terrorized them before leaving. The leader of that raiding party was another of our polished bright officers—Swadhin Kumar! And the vehicle he drove? Well, Suresh Bhatia's ambassador car. It was beneath him to sit in the rattling government-owned diesel jeep! And he was accompanied by the liquor dealer's agent. Where do we stand in this, Ajay? Can you see how deep this shamelessness of ours has spread its roots? Even after this, you can't refrain from making the "yours and mine" distinction?'

Ajay has been looking steadily at my face. When I stop, he sighs and shakes his head. Smilingly, he says, 'Uhf-f, you're so terribly emotional. All right, I agree, there's no distinction between my officers and yours. But, what was Stan doing there? From what I heard, isn't his project office near Kumardihi, at Satnala?'

'Orre Baba, from now on I'll have to ask him to travel with some sort of area permit from you. Stan was going for a meeting, to their head office in Delhi, and taking highway number forty-seven from Khamarpara cuts the journey to the airport by two hours. He saw a knot of Kureshpur women, and stopped to talk to them, and then because he waited for me Stan ended up missing the evening flight.'

'I've been told to keep watch on his movements, that's why I asked. You probably know him from before, right?'

Leaning my aching back on the seat, I looked at the small reading light overhead. It hasn't been working for some time. Without it, I can't read anything on a long night tour. Trying to read with a torch in one hand in a moving car is too difficult, and my time-beaten eyes start aching. Sanatan hasn't had the time to take the car to the garage for repair: because I never know when I'll have to go out, neither Sanatan nor the car get much rest. The two veins on the sides of my forehead are throbbing. From suppressed tension. Anger. Sorrow.

I respond to Ajayendra's question without looking at him, 'While studying at Osmania, Stan used to dabble in politics. Radical left. He was the students' union secretary when he was finishing his undergraduate degree. In Delhi too he was active in politics. I've known of him for the last four or five years, really only by name—we met for the first time only a year and a half ago at a friend's party. That's when I heard: he had joined a non-government organization, and would probably come to work in this area—well, aren't you making notes? Now you may have to keep a watch on me too from time to time.'

Rummaging through his pocket, Ajayendra brings out the empty cigarette packet. He feels cheated. By his calculation there should be two still in it. This imported brand waits in a carton on a shelf in his bedroom cupboard. Along this forest road it is impossible to get his favourite brand in any shop. Crumpling the packet and throwing it out of the window, Ajayendra says in a tone of deep sadness, 'I give up. It's impossible for me to carry on a conversation with you.'

That's quite all right. Let him stay silent. I too very much need to be by myself for a while. It will be midnight when we reach Mahuldiha. Somehow I'll have barely five hours of sleep. I've to sit down in the morning with a pile of files, I have to dictate a court verdict, and look into investigations and assorted matters. Having managed to half-block each of the arrows that Ajayendra has absently hurled at my conscience, and turn them back at him, even if not very consciously, I feel a kind of cruel joy. And why shouldn't I? Outwardly he's so seamlessly self-possessed, polished, bright, always correct and well-mannered—yet so fragile inside! Even a minor attack can break him. Why should I be the one always riddled inside with anger, misery? Whenever the sensitive person within me awakens, the ultimate weapons swiftly come at me from my environment 'Come on, you're so emotional!' 'Oh-ho Kamalika, you're not being objective, consider it with a cool head!' As though the responsibility for all the high-wire acts in this world is on my shoulders.

They're going to watch Stan D'Souza. Let them. While the world's arms dealers, owners of gambling rings, smugglers, food adulterers, go about in starched clean white collars and smooth smiles laid on a platter in the company of elite circles, and have a passport to cross any threshold, fixing someone's son's medical admission, someone else's daughter's trip abroad, here we'll pronounce the Stan D'Souzas guilty at the merest hint of suspicion and wash our hands clean. 'Everything about him is so very suspicious!' With an honours degree in physics, a management degree after that, a B.Tech. over and above, why does this fellow dress in homespun dhoti and kurta? What's his problem? Why the rough cotton wrapper on his shoulder? Why has he grown a beard? Going from village to village collecting facts on the lives and livelihoods of weavers, blacksmiths, potters and fisherfolk, writing down stuff in a thick notebook— does it add up to a credible occupation? He has set up office in a dusty, drought-parched village near Kumardihi, in a brick-walled structure, plastered but not yet colour-washed, roofed with tiles. This fellow is the project director. He sits in a communal kitchen with his workers on datepalm mats eating coarse-grained rice with curried eggplant. Eggplants are grown in Kumardihi throughout the year and they sell cheap. In a corner of the kitchen is a pile of eggplants. Why? He's training adivasi young men and women in building leadership qualities. What's the country going to do with so many leaders? Only one will win the election, after all. In the training camp the young men and women live and eat together without shame; when they've finished eating, they wash the pots and pans, store them in their place, and then enjoy themselves singing and dancing. What's this all about? O hey, middle-babu—the middle-babu isn't here?—Well then the junior-babu, come on now and find out what's going on—debauchery, or preparation for religious conversion? A young man, in good health, with a solid physique, and intelligent as well, why does he hang out here, languishing, what's his motive, how do you explain it? Go on, watch him, watch him and inform us.

That evening the young man had to miss the Delhi flight after all. He was going for an urgent meeting at their head office. Later he called me from the state capital. That night, sitting by the tamarind tree, I talked with him for quite some time. He thanked me for that. Expressed concern: will there be an investigation, punishment for the guilty, and will the investigation be objective?

'Where are you calling from, Stan?'

'From a public booth. Well, I've already told you these things, I'm calling now for a different reason.'

'What is it?'

'That night when you sat down with us in Khamarpara,

shortly before that some sort of message came for you written on a piece of paper. As you read it in that pale light the expression on your face changed, seemed as though you were in pain. Would you mind if I ask you what happened? After all, we held you up and delayed you.'

'Nothing much really. Now I don't quite remember either. Must have been something in the office. Don't spend your time at the phone booth any longer—you'll miss this flight too. We'll talk when we meet.'

'All right, we'll do that.' Stan put the telephone down.

What good would it have done to tell him about it? A sensitive, intelligent young man, he would've suffered too. A fishhook of pain caught in my throat—as it does so often, so often. I've suffered, my mind dashes headlong like a damaged airplane, but I have not a moment to myself. Quickly I spread a carpet of a sense of responsibility over the wreckage and get on to the task at hand! It's become a habit now. That day Animesh had despatched the news by wireless; and the police station had sent it to me on a piece of paper because I was out in the field. When I'm not in Mahuldiha, Animesh has to receive, and read, all the wireless messages and official letters, take my telephone calls, gauge their importance and communicate with me if necessary. The message that day was this: If you're returning via Kumardihi, then please stop by Lorka. Adil and his wife are dead. The labourers aren't releasing the bodies; there's been tension since last evening. The super says your visit will help, as it's to you that Adil was particularly....

Suicide. Not accident. Slipping a noose around her neck his wife hanged herself. Adil followed her. As I read that piece of paper in the weak light by the river bank, for a few seconds the world before me blanked out. At the time, Stan was standing in front of me, and behind him the wives and daughters of Kureshpur, whom, I hadn't at first noticed in the dark. But in that moment a sort of transparent barrier descended between us. I've failed to save Adil's life—my grief made me numb. Adil's bushy copper hair, his two large eyes dancing in amusement, the row of bright teeth, the lance-like lithe body came up and stood before me, all at once like the mist that comes up from the forest on winter evenings.

It was a Sunday. They materialised all of a sudden, without warning, at the end of Jaisthya, the heat searing the hillsides and stony highlands. The monsoon was yet to come—we waited for it every day. After the scattered showers of a fortnight ago, the farmers had run their ploughs once through the fields already. In the eighth month of the lean season from Magh to the end of Bhadra, until the short paddy comes off the fields, each day seems interminable to them. Their share of the crop finishes in just about two months following the sankranti festival, with its dancing and merrymaking. The main rice crop may still be far off, but there will be work on the creditors' fields. Even if they don't pay proper wages, they will at least give some rice. Or some leftovers of cooked rice! If the monsoon is erratic as it was the year before, then it will be a disaster. In this district, it doesn't rain after early Ashwin. If planting is delayed, the paddy will scorch before it matures. That's terribly painful, like having to stand by and watch your baby die in your arms.

Adil and his people, of course, didn't have to worry about the rain. All that ended in their fathers' lifetime—when having lost their land, they were reduced from small farmers to marginal farmers, farm labourers to mine labourers. This time even that last bit of ground under their feet was threatened. Wages had not been paid at the limestone quarries for a month and a half; the workers were sitting in dharna, demanding back wages. The top management had fled to Delhi, from where came frequent telexes and wires—it's on the way, give us a couple more days, and so on. Some junior officials were still around but almost all of them locked up their offices and disappeared. At first, the labour colony's grocery shop, paan shop and cut-piece cloth store would sell on credit—rice, lentils, oil, soap, paan and tobacco. But then, a rumour spread: the mine was closing down—and it slashed even those few lifelines. Supplies of limestone loaded in goods trains used to be sent regularly to the west of this state and to the neighbouring states. With obsolete equipment and not a penny spent on research for a very long time, the price per ton kept rising. As the price climbed, factories buying the limestone cut down on purchases, and payments were withheld because prices remained in dispute. Earlier, at the end of each week the company would have the previous week's accounts settled. This now started to take upto a month, to the alarm of the head office. The factories were then instructed not to make payments to Lorka—'Send the money here, to the Delhi branch, we'll judge the situation and settle whatever is due from here.' The cost increase, the underutilization of equipment in all that cobweb of hazy economics in the talks and discussions among the secretaries of the steel, coal and industry ministries—on these hung the future of 250 labourers, supervisors and other dispensable human lives.

Adil had stepped forward, smiling, from the crowd. 'Are you afraid, Hakim-saheb?' He said to me, 'This is just my tangi, it's always with me, but look, both my hands are empty.' His words were followed by the laughter of all the young men and women with him—some 150-200 of them. Almost all of them had a tangi perched on their shoulders like a pet bird, or held a bamboo pole in their hands. Where did so many people come from? It was a holiday, I wasn't due to sit in court that day. I was going to stay home and do the files. I had a late bath, my wet hair hung loose on my back, still undone. I hurried out in the homespun kurta-pyjama I had on, my feet in home slippers, because Animesh looked terrified. Animesh had just done something he never does— knocked on my bedroom door.

His face pale and alarmed, he said, 'Madam, a large mob, armed, I've no idea from where. Shall I call the police station? Or shall I say you are not in? Whatever we do, we must do at once.'

Well, the suggestion was interesting. I could escape the back door of my own home—Animesh would go out and tell them that I wasn't in. The police headquarters has two sections of lathi-armed police on reserve, once called in they'd of course give their lives to save us from harm. They're mindful enough of their duty and responsibility. But this is an everyday problem for me. The door to this house is never closed, there are no guards posted outside. Just as on the first day of each new year the blind-mute and deaf children form a line and come straight in with bouquets of grasses, leaves and flowers, so does a mad crowd straight from the football ground in blind fury at the referee's decision. Where can I go to escape from this reality of mine?

Not many were home at that time. The sun was sharp. In a corner of the veranda Kuki sat on a mat playing with Basumati. Sanatan and Animesh were in the front room. Sanatan had thoughtfully put the car in the garage—any damage caused to the car because of the driver's negligence would mean a deduction from his salary. There were no sounds of things being smashed outside, no shouts or slogans, the men and women stood quietly, waiting, in the strong sun. I asked them in under the covered veranda, and for a couple of hours we talked of the mine's future and they all drank water with their cupped palms, and ate the gur and the batashas that Sanatan brought from Sibu Samanta's store. Then the rented trucks in which Adil and his people had come took them back to Lorka. It was on that day that I saw Adil's wife for the first time. In a maroon printed sari, a yellow blouse, with a wilted bunch of basak flowers in her hair, she stood very close to Adil and studied me with a slight smile lifting the corner of her mouth. A switch of unoiled copper-coloured hair curled onto her cheek.

The large army went back, happy with the assurance of some intervention on my part. After that, with the pressures we exerted, they did get two weeks' overdue wages. It did not occur to me that the sudden kindness was the flaring of an oil lamp just before it goes out. Suddenly one day, harried as I was with the pressure of work, the first intimation of the mine's closure arrived on my table. That young man, sharp as a spear-head, his young wife, sunlit like a spring flower, so soon they became history.

Standing in that dim light and reading the message sent by Animesh, I was thinking of the bodies that had not been cremated for twenty-four hours. The workers were refusing to release them. Soon they would start decomposing, the crowd's fury would grow worse, and…

It was late that night but I went on to Lorka. After leaving Stan and his group near the crossing of Khamarpara, I went

on because it was extremely important for me to convey to
Adil, to the dead Adil and his living friends that I wasn't
afraid, that I didn't want to run away from them.

4

⬥

The town of Mahuldiha, or the large village known by that name, has a smell all its own. A primeval smell. Rather like the intoxicating fragrance that emanates from the giant body of the hill and the saal forests after their first soak of the monsoon. An eager, restless fragrance, the smell of a doe's body that arouses the spotted stag on a moonlit night. The smell that rises after midnight from mahuls falling on dying embers of a ring of limited fire made earlier along the edge of the hill. There's no name for this smell, it has no physical identity. Yet one who senses of this fragrance doesn't fail to 'feel' it. Why else would that great big bear come out of the Kanika forest, forgetful of his usual track, and come into this town; there is no logic to his straying here! We can safely presume that the petrol-pump owner Abadh Singh has never caught this smell, nor has Santosh Ray the moneylender, not even the local cooperative bank's president Taraknath Dehuri. Yet they've been in this place for some three generations now. They stay right here, morning and evening, filling their gagris without getting their hair wet, because here it's possible to loot and give nothing in return. Taraknath Dehuri himself had told me the story of how

Mahuldiha—a long strip which tapers in the middle before spreading south—came to be the district headquarters when actually Kumardihi, an industrial town, had the first claim. The limestone quarries of Lorka, the iron-ore mines of Chiri, more or less surround Kumardihi.

Kumardihi has a much larger population. Plenty of schools and colleges, cinema halls and hotels there. Recently, several clubs and swimming pools have come up, adding to the town's attraction. But, quite apart from the asphalt roads lined with the shimmering shades of acacias in residential colonies, thanks to the industries there, the geographical location of Kumardihi places it right at the centre of the district. By comparison, Mahuldiha is at the very northwest corner, edging the district boundary; the town municipality's billboard of welcome comes after the rickety bridge on the Jhima river has been crossed. Mahuldiha has nothing much, just a rainbow- stamped past. Right after Independence, it became the district town, the way an over-the-hill senior queen takes the ceremonial seat, and carried on more or less proudly for some ten years. It was then that the petrol pump, the poultry farm, the cinema hall and the rows of shops came up by the town's entrance. The bus depot got built, the government college, the playground-park. The vegetable market's evening bustle, the warehouse of kendu and saal leaves—these were the meagre signs of Mahuldiha's commerce. Mahuldiha was once, from 1711 until the Battle of Plassey, the centre of the estate of Balarampur, during the times of the Rajahs Ananta Chaudhuri and Basanta Chaudhuri. In 1850, a new palace was built atop the mound. It can be seen from afar. Almost twenty-two acres of it—with an audience hall, inner quarters, temple pavilion, the running wall, all prominently visible—in a dull-sunshine yellow earlier, recently painted white by Ranadeb Chaudhuri. The rajas are no more, nor their rajatva, but there is Ranadeb Kumar Bahadur or the 'Kumar-saheb', and his wife Anangamanjari still referred to as Rani by the villagers. The old palace, made of mud and stone, stood beyond the city limits. It's crumbled now except for the remnants of a few walls. They call it the *garh* of Nayanpur. Now goats graze there, and vagabond boys fly multi-coloured kites.

Ranadeb Chaudhuri's father passed away some years ago. Decayed from excessive drinking, he spent the last few years lying wasted, on his bed. But while he was in his heyday, he kept fighting for Mahuldiha. At the start of the sixties, however, once work on the steel mill began, the scales tipped in favour of Kumardihi. Rumour had it that the district-headquarters would move to Kumardihi. The construction of a shopping complex on prime land next to Harish Ray Road was suddenly stopped—it was said that a team was coming to Kumardihi to pick land for the civil court and that the district magistrate had already selected a spot for the bungalow. Enough! The advocates of Mahuldiha called a strike, and Mahadeb Chaudhuri got out on to the road, joining hands with the opposition party. There was a flood of protest: from the schoolchildren, the shopkeepers, the villagers at this end, ordinary 'subjects' to come to the court and the offices. It's like that story of a father who slapped his son, saying, 'Watch it, don't break that plate,' because it would be useless to slap him once the plate was broken. In the capital the chief minister wore a slight frown; the right noises were made: nothing has been decided yet, the cabinet hasn't discussed it, the Bidhan Sabha hasn't debated on it—what's all this childish agitation about?

Taraknath Dehuri ended this narration by wiping his moustaches with a deep pink, girlish handkerchief, saying, 'Who can tell what each one held in his heart at the time?' Ah, the way he put it sounded almost like a line from a song.

Yes, Mahadeb Chaudhuri won. Mahuldiha remained the district headquarters. But Mahuldiha's economy never took off, much like the growth of an undernourished child. Beyond a sawmill or two that came up initially, there were no factories, no further growth of commerce. The town became more and more dirty and dilapidated by the day, no wonder, with the municipality in such bad shape. 'We oldtimers watch this and sigh, you see—our life, death everything is here. We'll never leave Mahuldiha and go to Kumardihi. That would be like going against our dharma.'

'It would indeed,' solemnly I agreed with Taraknath-babu. How unhesitatingly people bring out religion, like a filthy handkerchief from their pockets.

Taraknath's wife Minati wears gold jewellery, her arms covered from wrist to elbow. Taraknath keeps several women in the nearby villages of Agharias and Mahatos. Besides, where could he go, this man in baggy shorts with talismans round his neck, leaving his many offspring and the fifty bighas of prime paddy lowland he owns in defiance of the land ceiling law? After a certain age the weariness in a man's bones starts eating at him from the inside. This silk kurta, the thick gold chain around his neck, the smell of essence in his pink handkerchief—at his age can these things be matched in the industrial capital of Kumardihi? The Kumardihi elite are different in every way. In the evening parties held at clubs, or at swimming pool barbecues, Taraknath Dehuri or moneylender Santosh Ray would be totally out of place with their bald heads or oiled hair, their moustaches twirled up or razor-trimmed, their silk kurtas or gaberdine pants. The fascinating way of sipping lightly from a glass, the sparklers of English words, is it possible to learn these things at the fag end of life? Work on the steel mill's second phase will soon begin, the tenders are out. The foreign-returned engineers sweating from the heat even in their tee shirts, the management units all brand new, polished, the slim youths who are second-generation industrialists, the ravishing lipsticked wives of the colony's officers—they're all quite determined to collectively take Kumardihi into the new century.

Santosh Ray, bald-headed, jelly-bellied, always dressed in shabby pyjama bottoms and a terrycot shirt as an integral part of his battle plan, has his nose in a constant twist just from the effort of holding up his glasses. However, he has hidden his bit of discontent like an enamel eroded tooth. People address him as mahajan, while they address Dehuri-babu as 'president'. Peeled, both onions are quite the same. On paper, of course, Santosh-babu also owns a cold-storage unit or two and no less than two cinema halls. Just as Taraknath Dehuri is the president of the cooperative bank on paper, and runs a business giving compound-interest loans from home. The cooperative bank's complicated, roundabout business methods, done with paper and pen, have a twisted relationship with the business conducted from home without pens and account books. The twists might be possible to unravel if a video camera was aimed non-stop at each of the characters involved. Otherwise, no amount of poring over inspection reports will solve this puzzle.

Suppose Madan Ghasi applies to the bank for a loan to buy a pair of bullocks. The amount that the application form shows is four thousand five hundred rupees, the form has been filled in by a young chap, the secretary's chela, who

charges ten rupees for filling it and fifty for recording it in
the files. Not right then, but to be deducted when the money
is given. The secretary will scribble: 'Four thousand may be
granted.' President Dehuri's, pen has the final say, and he
considers it: This fellow has been sharecropping all these
years and now, just because the cauliflower and tomato prices
have gone up for two successive years, he's claiming that…
be that as it may, the amount granted is three thousand and
five hundred rupees. Pay him in two instalments or the chap
may squander all that money drinking and doing who knows
what. Release three thousand initially; let the chap bring the
receipt for what he bought with the first fifteen hundred,
and only then will the other fifteen hundred be given. Of
course, included in this sum is a government subsidy of one
thousand rupees. Well, no matter whether it comes from
the government or belongs to Dehuri-babu, is it something
to throw away? After making two trips to the cattle market
to select his bullocks, Madan Ghasi comes back, apologetic.
No one sells just one bullock, both must be bought together,
he says. At the cash counter, Mallik-babu is not one to give
in easily. 'How can you take out three thousand at once?
Are you crazy?' In this way spring rolls into early summer,
Jaisthya goes by and Asharh comes, and Madan Ghasi has
gone to the cooperative bank eighteen times, having to spend
two hundred and fifty rupees on transport and another thirty
on tea and snacks. Luckily he doesn't even have shoes, or the
soles would've given way long ago. This time, watching the
clouds darkening in the sky, Madan becomes anxious. It's
six months since he got the plot of land high on the hillside
out of the surplus over land ceiling. The plot is pulling him.
Whenever he is sober, the stony land under the babla shrubs
seems to beckon. That's why, like a good boy, Madan finally

goes to Dehuri-babu's house, following the advice of the cooperative society's secretary, gets a loan of the full four thousand rupees to buy the bullocks from a wholesaler known to Dehuri-babu. The money carries a steep rate of interest of course, but better that than lose the rainy season. The year after next, Madan's bullocks will go back to the wholesaler, they're bound to, because even though Madan has repaid the instalments, by some supernatural calculation, the interest has come to exceed the principal. 'See Madan, this is precisely why I do business with people I know; you're known to me, so is Ramjan Mian.' After that, Madan goes again to the cooperative society with a fallen face. He goes there only to learn that for those like him who did not take the loan after it was granted, no application will be accepted for the next three years. Dehuri sounds genuinely worried when he asks me, 'Can you tell me why the cooperative movement has not worked in this country? It's really the people's attitude, you know, we run after them with the money, but do they care? Village after village is ruined because these people are addicted to alcohol.'

They're like wolves, or jackals, who live on the blood of human beings, not of inferior creatures. They thrive, they multiply, and that great big confused bear from the Kanika forest, that poor thing just died. As terror and anxiety spread through the town, and anxious villagers started hanging around the palace compound, Kumar Bahadur Ranadeb Chaudhuri appeared at my doorstep one Chaitra evening. Usually, if there's anything specific to be discussed, we talk on the phone. He rarely comes to see me.

'What can I do when my subjects are anxious,' he says, 'And I too have a special responsibility, perhaps I should finish off the beast, what do you say?'

The reek of his perfume is hideous, and the smell of liquor and sweat too. How his head manages to sit atop his trunk without the help of a neck, that in itself is an anthropomorphic wonder! But this is no time to fuss about his perfume or wonder about his physique.

'The animal isn't doing any harm, it has been hemmed in, we're trying to catch it and return it to the jungle. If you kill it, you will violate the law.'

'The law? How can you say that? Whose law? The beast is from my forest, the gun is mine, and my killing it will be illegal—when my subjects are begging me for it!'

Perhaps he wanted a photo of himself with a foot on the dead bear. This sort of photo comes in handy in election campaigns too, young village women look at it wide-eyed. I heard this man once studied at Cambridge. If only I could make him disappear by blowing hard!

'I am busy right now. There's no other problem, is there?'

'There's just this one life-or-death problem, but you can't seem to solve even that, so why ask if there are others— huhn?,' Ranadeb Chaudhuri got up, making an awful screech with the chair. 'I'll do what I think is right, I'm just letting you know, that's all.'

'Be prepared then for the consequences, I'm just letting you know.'

Is burning coal this red? Pausing at the door, Mahadeb Chaudhuri's son glared at me, his eyes red with anger, for about twenty seconds. His retinue of followers held their collective breath, and I said, 'I don't like threatening eyes, Mr Chaudhuri. Let me not have to say this a second time.'

Then I asked for Rajat Iyer on the phone. He's the divisional forest officer.

The bear had strayed here from the Kanika forest, trampling underfoot the bamboo shoots, the flowering wild datura shrubs, the weaver-bird nests which fell off trees. How did it manage to negotiate the many curves and bends along the way and come so close to Mahuldiha? Just outside the forest, in the village of Sisamtarh on the slope, the poor animal was confronted with the first of the ferocious collective chases by humans. They came after it with tangis, thick poles, flaming torches of oil-soaked rags tied on sticks, they came shouting, making loud noises. What they did was only natural because no one had ever imagined having to face a bear come out and stand before you at midday under the scorching sun while you are heading home with the plough across paddy fields. For a whole day and night the bear kept running. Hunger blazed in its stomach, mounting rage and frustration butted inside its head; in the village of the Mahatos, escaping downhill, it struck a paw at the shoulder of a small boy, shredding his tender body in the process. This time the tangis took revenge on its body, struck at its back and raised forelegs. Everything now became confused for the bloodied bear— its calculations of the route, the destination, why it was running. This time it attacked anyone it found in its path, and was attacked in turn, the ferocity of the chase infecting its bloodstream with a kind of blind fear.

Going up north beyond the Mahuldiha city limits, to the right of the road, there are bare rocky hillsides stretching far. Close to the horizon the soft silhouette of the Kerandimal hills, over whose brows the sun sets. The hazy saal forests lying at the foot of the hills are perhaps where the bear was headed in its attempt to hide. But it did not manage to do that. Instead it kept lifting its nose in the air, trying to catch the smell of something, and in the process, quickly moved towards a white building, faintly visible in the gray twilight. The chief of the social forestry division had rented that house three years ago, no one quite knows why. Perhaps simply because the rent was low. It was far from the city, not well-connected by bus and the office staff had a lot of trouble getting there. So they were all unhappy in that office. Of course, at duskfall on that day, almost no one was in, the babus had left before five to catch the bus. The building's front door was wide open, the iron gate outside was not closed either. Because this was the time when the chowkidar checked whether the lights and fans had been switched off. He'd then close up the windows and doors and lock the front door. Standing in the dim interior of a back room, he noticed the agitated bear from a window between two rooms. A native Kandh, that adivasi youth quietly went out the back door and locked the building from outside. On the main road, by then, the eager, aggressive crowd pursuing it had stopped. Seeing the hall's tables and chairs, typewriters and almirahs before him, the bear suddenly realized that it hadn't come to the right place. Its head was still heavy, filled with smoke. The iron gate outside had been locked; but the unrelenting noise of shouting, whistling, drumming on tins filled its ears.

Very quickly Rajat took a decision. Before stationing armed guards on all sides, he had the exit securely blocked with thick strong netting. In the meantime the building's front door had also been locked. Inside, it was dark. Driven all night by hunger and pain from the wounds, the bear had ransacked the hall, and the office. Two typewriters fell onto the floor, bunches of paper were torn and scattered, the almirah damaged with clawmarks. The bear butted its head and shoulders against the door, the sound of which had alerted the gun-carrying guards stationed outside. Finally, towards the close of the second day, this unequal war came to an end. After a long period of silence, when everyone assumed it had given up or fallen asleep, the bear crashed through the front door with its inhuman strength and as it came running out, got caught in the net of thick nylon ropes. Of course, it could not be allowed to live—it might attack again, so a bullet was fired through its chest. Then two or three more were sent into the throat and abdomen.

Shortly before the post-mortem at the veterinary hospital, Rajat and I went and looked at the bear. Close to six feet tall, a huge ferocious creature, froth still at the corners of its mouth, yet bloodied and helpless, it was covered in dust, as lifeless and unalterable as history. The office resembled a battlefield. Everyone went away and they closed the office for an indefinite period. The burra saheb was going through the books trying to find out who could be made to pay for the repairs—the landlord, the social forestry division, or Rajat—because presumably it was Rajat's fault that this bear came out of the forest at all.

Rajat was showing me the state of the bars of the small window in the back room; all bent and twisted. 'Think of the strength in his body, he did this with his paws.'

'But he still couldn't make it, Rajat, he lost.' Looking at those bars, I was reminded of my childhood. How that little Babli, watching the red flood of sunset, had wanted to bend the bars just like this and fly away. But she couldn't. And she still has her feet fixed to the ground, still nursing within her the wounds inflicted by various weapons.

'Oh, the torment of the last twenty-four hours!' said Rajat. 'If the bear had escaped somehow, and attacked someone, I'd have been in real trouble. And then there were Kumar

Bahadur's antics going on the whole time! It's lucky you
weren't away somewhere. I was worried about that—that's
why I got your written order beforehand! Without that we
couldn't have taken him—'

Taking my eyes off the red sun setting over the Kerandimal
hill, I turned to Rajat and smiled sadly, 'You did the right
thing.'

On the way back we passed the octroi check gate. Atop
a small mound on its left is a single mahul tree. It looks so
enchanting in the twilight. I've seen this tree in all kinds
of light. After sunrise, in the middle of the day—when the
sun is burning bright, and when, bathed in moonlight, she
is like a solitary woman in a pond with her tresses spread
out in the placid water. It's a very old tree, with all sorts of
knots all over her body, her arid bark is a grayish colour, even
the branches sort of bend and twist to look up towards the
sky. But to really see her, one has to see her as a whole, the
trunk, the branches, the clusters of leaves, all together, from
very far, when she seems like a dream in green and yellow,
beckoning. The breadth of the branches and foliage is truly
immense because of her age. Somehow it seems that this tree
was what gave the village its name—Mahuldiha—perhaps
many hundred years ago. Because in this locality there is no
other mahul tree left, the others that used to be here are gone,
roots and all. A long time ago this area had all belonged to
the Mundas, the Oraons, the Kandhs and the Juangs, who
are the original children of this soil. Through the ages, kings
have come and gone, but the central stream of their way of
life remained the same. Each local community's own pahan,
mahato and bhandari headed the hatu or village panchayat,
their own dishari did the spirit healing, their own panchayats
exiled or fined individuals, or decided to forgive the guilty, to

welcome them back with song and dance, provided they were prepared to pay a fine in liquor.

Each community here has various sub-communities, with their own rules and customs. The dances and songs, the prayers and festivals, the marriage customs, the way their homes are set up—everything is different. The Juangs have one system of cultivation, the Mundas another. In the last half century, even though the material aspects of their lives changed rapidly, their beliefs, culture and social ties have flowed in secluded streams, as self-contained as before.

The first big shock these people experienced was when British rule was established. It was then that the revenue-collecting zamindars came into the picture, viewing the adivasi social leaders with suspicion and distrust. Gradually trade opened up, train and road transport came close to their villages. In place of the easy, direct arithmetic of buying salt, onions or dried fish in exchange for roots and vegetables, came cash accounts. As a result the tribals have been cheated in cash transactions; and when traders from other states come in the dry season to sell tobacco, chillies, kerosene and salt and leave with oxcarts loaded with freshly harvested crops worth twice as much, then they're beaten in barter trade as well. Their debts have grown at compound interest rates. Thus, gradually they lost their land, had to sell the plough and the bullocks, and finally they had to accept the life of landless wage-labourers.

In 1930 some two-thirds of the land in the village was owned by tribals. Half a century later, there is not an inch of space for them. Take the case of Belangi, a village just about two miles from Mahuldiha. Only four acres of all paddy lowlands there are with adivasis, 375 acres are owned by others; the ratio on the dry highlands is the opposite—a

150 acres are adivasi-owned and just 29 are owned by others. The highlands are without irrigation, their yield of rice dependent on uncertain rainfall and often very low. But this is the plight of those who own land. Others like Bigna Munda, Dukhu Oraon, Hasu Kharia, whose hunting trips once sent shivers through these hill forests, are now reduced to bonded labourers.

Once the police stations, the courts and offices came in and took root, the traditional panchayats fell apart. Even the adivasis now mostly run to the courts to report theft or murder. Since independence, panchayats set up by the government have challenged the informal system of the hatu, toli and parba panchayats. Earlier, people would appeal against the decision of a hatu or village panchayat to the higher parha panchayat; harsh penalties like exile could be ruled only by the parha; the responsibility for resolving all disputes, from the accounts of village grain stock to the case of an unmarried girl's abduction, rested with the adivasi panchayats.

But, like an atrophied limb deprieved of blood, the heart of the adivasis' social life has gradually been deprived of sustenance by trade and commerce, industry and the gamut of law-based institutions. As a result, the tribals have lost their society and have gained little in terms of livelihood. So many of them fought in the battle for independence that it's no surprise to find village plaques commemorating martyrs by the side of small roads even today, small boys pointing out a martyr's home, or the place his blood had spilled. After independence, it took a little while for the realization to sink in that their battle was not over, only the parties had changed. There are laws and the courts, there are development plans, seed supplies, bankloans, wells, motor pumps, tractor cooperatives, but even now one careless step can get you into trouble—even things you can claim by right have to be fought for. The lives of the tribals are still tied by invisible strings to the goti-malik they were bonded to the creditors, the sahukars who promised them everything and then bled them dry. Now their sons and grandsons are in the cooperative bank, the ration shop, the tractor rental business, and when they have problems they have no recourse except to run to their former malik's backdoor. And yet, by law, no adivasi land is supposed to change hands without the district magistrate's permission.

Delving into a case of illegal land transfer would produce a Mahabharata. The illegal buyer is too clever to transfer the land to his name. He simply uses it, taking the crop from it after the harvest, and he can never be traced. In court, even the adivasis will deny any illegal transfer, because standing across from them is the buyer's man, the one at whose door they'll have to knock to be able to survive from Chaitra to Bhadra each year. In this terrible darkness there is, however, a ray of hope. More than a hundred adivasi cooperative societies have begun to keep their own accounts of crops and irrigation water, sending out harvests to sell; Ajayendra and I have worked as a team to catch usurious creditors on grounds of extortion instead of relying on toothless, clawless legalities; Stan and his group are at work. He's new in this. But there's the Adivasi Mukti Bahini, the Banabasi Sangha doing the groundwork of organizing since years. The changes are minute; it takes a whole generation before even the beginnings of change become visible. They had so much, they've lost so much—perhaps they'll regain some of it. But, just like rehabilitating the landless Bishai Munda of the riverbank shack, bringing back the mahul trees will remain an impossible socio-economic feat.

But I've got sidetracked. An adivasi would die rather than

cut a living mahul. Mahul fruit and flowers keep them alive through the year. Not just the drink from fermented flowers but during summer many families live for days on the fruit cooked in water. Sadly, the affluent farmers and traders who came from other states or moved from other districts of the state into an adivasi district, have never felt any such concern for these trees—for forests in general or for the relationship between people and forests. Muhuldiha businessmen run illegal log-selling operations in the Kanika, Rampur and Belangdihi forests. The profits from this inter-state log-smuggling flow into their homes and pockets, while hundreds of nearly naked starving people—adivasi, harijan, landless—get caught by the railway police, the forest guards and armed police for taking a mere headload. With similar callousness, the outsiders have eliminated the mahul trees that had once filled this rural town; they've opened licensed liquor shops, set up rows of potsherd-roofed huts where they run businesses selling the 'services' of adolescent girls procured from the villages. That lone tree on the hillock has somehow survived. It has seen much and has aged inside, but it has not died. May it go on living as an icon of the dream of Bishai sitting by the river two hundred miles from here at the other end of the district, of the dreams of the martyrs Sudhir Munda and Lakhan Nayek! That's why on my way in and out, in light and darkness, I look at this tree again and again with love and hope.

Beyond the check gate, some way down the tarred road, is the police line on the right and then the main police station. After that, the hospital, the irrigation department store, the drinking water suppliers' office, in front of which two or three old tankers sit through rain and sun, then there's the municipality. Similar buildings all of a yellowish colour, like books in worn brown-paper covers in a row. After the traffic light, farther down on the left is the children's park built by the municipality. The trees are dusty, water-deprived, unkempt, and the pond has been besieged by water hyacinths. On the right are the government quarters, at their back a parallel road edged by the staff colony. At the crossroads beyond this lies the new market on its east and west. New only in name, the market was built some thirty years ago, made up of cement walls topped by tin roofs. Inside, there are hair-cutting saloons, tailors, paan shops, cut-piece shops, a variety of grocery stores, a restaurant and a video rental shop that has sprouted recently. Just behind this market area is the temple ground, mandir-tala, where the Saturday haat gathers. In the old map of the mouza, a map supposedly made in the year 1880, it is exactly this site that is listed as the haat. Amazing! Even though a hundred years have passed, people—their sons, grandsons, granddaughters-in-law, relatives of later generations—have been coming here in the same way for their weekly shopping needs.

The haat-tala has quite a few large trees—banyan, peepul, saal. Under the banyan is the temple of Chandi—there's no idol there, only a big black stone, the original features of which are obscured by many years of dabbed vermilion, sprinkled water and uncooked rice offerings. It is clear that this one is not the shakta Hindu goddess Chandi, but a deity of the Mundas and Oraons. I've heard that both communities in this area used to worship Chandi before going out hunting, and the deity used to stay in the home of their pahanov chief. Perhaps the pahan's home was right here. About twenty years ago an old clerk from Ranadeb Chaudhuri's estate office built a little temple over this stone. The forest was once quite close by. Under attack from human greed, the forest has retreated. The trees were more or less driven off, and even this stone appropriated by the very same greed. A bare-chested unemployed young Brahmin wearing a tuft at the back of his shaved head, his sacred thread atop a worn silk dhoti, sits in the porch of the temple, counting up the coin offerings and sprinkling visitors to the haat with flower petals dipped in murky water. He also collects a few rupees from fearful young wives and daughters, ostensibly to protect them from evil by performing some rituals. Unless very carefully scrutinized, there's not much difference between this haat in Mahuldiha town and many others in the district. I may not have mentioned this before, but the district too is named Mahuldiha after the town. The village haat grounds are often located between two villages, usually bordering a road used by buses and trucks. The town's haat is surrounded by regular stores and buildings crowding around it. In other places it's different—with a mountain stream or tilled fields or deep forests around.

This Saturday market in Mahuldiha is large; traders from virtually all villages within a ten-mile radius come here. In this region, some haats are held on Tuesdays, some on Wednesdays, some on Saturdays. People from one village probably have access to two or three haats within four or five miles if there are other villages close by. In the extensive area between the Kerandimal and the Mahavir hills, the villages are isolated from each other. The two rivers Jhima and Champajharan and the Sarang ditch surround each one's panchayat with irregular water boundaries. The people there, especially the tribes that live up in the hills, have to walk twelve to fifteen miles to go to the haat. But what will they buy there? And what will they buy it with? A little salt, some karanja plums, a quarter bottle of sesame or mustard oil, a half litre of kerosene maybe, some dry chillies, at the most a cheap poplin shirt, an identical pair of millmade saris, and that too only on festive occasions or just after the harvest. In winter evenings, when smoke from stovefires slowly rises above the lightless shanties to blend in the mist, and darkness falls abruptly on the hills around, perhaps the moon rises, an angry red paper lantern of a moon and in the liquid moonlight which dilutes the thick blood of darkness, people can be seen returning from the haat. A young woman with a small basket of provisions on her head, a suckling baby in a piece of cloth tied across her back, asleep against the warmth of her mother's body. A young man on whose head something sits on coiled straw, perhaps a large ripe pumpkin being taken back unsold, on one shoulder an empty pot, and on the other a slightly older naked child. Man and woman are both somewhat tipsy: they've drunk mahul or rice liquor using the leftover rice they brought along. They're singing loudly, their steps landing unevenly, as they keep walking. A weekly market, whether in Mahuldiha or any other town, is not just a place for people to buy and sell, it's a place for socializing, to talk about joys and sorrows, to discuss the course of the drought. Someone sighs for the bullock that died. The Oraon youth who, in love with a girl from his own clan, has set up home in exile, also comes to the marketplace. While he's buying paan, his girl, having deliberately drifted through the crowd, squats before the fancy-goods shop, fingering the colourful combs, silk hair ribbons and strings of plastic beads. The trader from some other land barks at her, 'Why do you touch things for nothing? Are you buying anything?'

The girl asks, 'How much is this string of beads?'

'Two and a half rupees. Can you pay? If not, don't touch anything.'

The girl pulls in her hand. The eager-bright dark face goes out at once. From the last week's haat her lover got her a red blouse. That string of red pea-round beads would've been perfect with it. But where's she going to get two and a half rupees?

Motilal the bania, and also a bania's son, turns his face aside and puffs at the nearly finished bidi, smiling to himself. It's his business to draw in these helpless insects like a spider by showing them the shiny dewdrops swaying in its gossamer net. The girl is beautiful, large-eyed, her waist can be circled between two hands; even in the worn-out discoloured sari she looks tender and fresh like wet neem leaves. The lovers are exiles from the village of Khapia. Motilal could give her the string of beads free if he could briefly have her alone at duskfall. But Lagnu Oraon, that companion of hers, might someday find Motilal on a deserted road and use the tangi to lop his head off! He'd then be losing his head as well as the string of beads. Far pleasanter to just sit here and take in the firm bends, the hills and valleys of young girls' bodies, seek out the primitive smell of freshly rained-on earth from their necks and foreheads. After all, you can't have everything.

At the small haats, traders bring their goods in bullock carts, or in tractors. Some carry bundles of clothes or light plastic things on their heads. Once in a while there's a cattle market. Hundreds of bullocks, and cows sit or stand here and there haphazardly. Prospective buyers negotiate prices, check out horns, count up the teeth.

This kind of sprawling market is found in areas close to villages where the panchayats are located. For a pair of bullocks that cost no more than 3,000 rupees, Manjur Mian quotes 12,500, letting the babus hovering around do their show-haggling. The price is brought down to 4,300, after which the 1,300 are divided up in silence, and out of sight. On the books the loan is of 4,300 to Budhbari Mundain, widow of Suka Munda, address Jamtali, panchayat Lamta; the transaction paper is signed by the panchayat secretary. Taking Budhbari's thumb and vigorously rubbing it on the stamp pad, the Block office clerk Amulya-babu says, 'Believe me, you were born with luck. We don't give loans to widows. The one in whose name the land is, departed to heaven, and you a woman will till the land and repay the loan!' Embarrassed to be breaking official convention and by her own helplessness, Budhbari smiles stupidly, rubbing the released finger's purple stain on her dry hair. Manjur Mian smiles. The field officer smiles too. Their smiles all have different meanings.

At a large haat like this are rows of trucks that arrive by the national highway. From the neighbouring states come vegetables—tomatoes, eggplants, banana clusters on the stem—and eggs that local wholesalers buy. In their turn, they sell the local crops—huge green jackfruits, mangoes, dry chillies, turmeric, bought cheaply from villagers through agents. On the haat day the noise of the crowd is so much you can't hear a thing. Once in a while haggling turns into fighting. Amidst all this, mikes amplify throat-splitting voices selling tooth powder, five-herb extract, lottery tickets. At the forest department stall, lots of saplings are sold before the rains; now a firewood depot has also opened. The hot kachauris, samosas and jalebis being fried in rapeseed oil spread their irresistible aroma in the afternoon sky. A shameless ox trying to sneak a mouthful from the vegetable baskets is turned away with a raised stick.

Beyond the temple ground's invisible boundary are colonies number eight and number nine, the town's most destitute and dirty areas. Hard to say how these wards got their numbers; ward number seven next to three, five next to one. But number nine is correctly placed next to number eight, the one for harijans, the other for adivasis. As one leaves the tarred road behind and enters the slum, one can see rows of mud huts, roofed in tin or shards of tiles. A few have masonry walls, using lime and brick-dust instead of cement. The unpaved lane winds its way between the rows. There are no proper drains. The overflow of tubewell water flows on the lane, forming pools of muddy and smelly water. There's a street light at the head of the main lane, it glows dimly when there's a bulb in it. Some homes now have low-cost electric connections under the city development plan, but most are dark. Oil is expensive; kerosene they need for cooking because collecting firewood is very difficult in an urban area like this. Few can afford to dispel the night's darkness with an oil or kerosene lamp. The harijans are almost all landless daily-wage labourers—they work in Mahuldiha's bazaar area or in nearby villages. Some adivasi families have land; a few others have a member in low-grade office jobs and some are day labourers. They are descendants of those original inhabitants of Mahuldiha who held their heads high three hundred years ago, who were kings of the hills and forests here. Most have gone away, having lost the economic battle and sold their land. Those who've stayed on survive by begging creditors for concessions—on the basis of old connections they had as debtor, bonded labourer or sharecropper—and they wait for the day when their sons or daughters may manage to land a job as a peon or watchman in some government or private office or in a shop. Walking through these lanes in daytime, one sees naked babies crawling in courtyards, women picking lice off each other's hair, some sitting with shredded tobacco and a bunch of bidi leaves—the bidi factory agent will come in the evening, pay their wage and collect the bidis. The children go to the primary school. Despite the school's condition, enrolment has increased in the last twenty years. However, so many of them drop out before they finish middle school—some leave to herd goats, the girls to collect cowdung or help their mothers queue up for water or take care of children, the boys to wait at tables and wash dishes in food stalls and tea shops. Being harijans and adivasis, they will have jobs 'reserved' for them, but who can wait that long? Each new day, under the whip of hunger, disease and indigence, seems unending. The men age prematurely, their lungs eaten by tuberculosis; the women lose their loveliness and turn into ugly crones; the prostitutes are riddled with venereal disease even before their youthful glow has faded. Yes, businessmen visit here from outside, men from other villages, and yes, the endlessly virile truck drivers from states in the north and south also frequent this place. The shacks edging the haat are a lure for the young indigent girls of these two wards, fresh supplies of female flesh to meet the growing demand.

After the haat is over, I have often wandered in this vacant, dismantled spot in the hazy darkness just after twilight. It feels strange. The chill of a deserted battlefield underfoot. Rotten leaves, ragged gunny bag pieces, discarded baskets lying around, spots where a little earlier the air was thick with laughter and jokes, with fragments of conversation and catcalls, or with the smell of bidis, are now in boundless silence. This Mahuldiha village-town of ours will continue to sit by the roadside like a child. Kumardihi will grow in wealth and prestige day by day even though it'll be only the favourite, not the seniormost.

Here too, elections will come treading softly like dry leaves following the wind. Every vertical surface from bamboo-mat walls to cement masonry will get plastered with posters. The acolytes of Ranadeb Chaudhuri, who himself doesn't contest but runs things by 'supporting' the party candidate, will be out collecting their 'taxes'. And the chairman of the municipality, Vikram Sardar, will come on stage in his mild and bland manner. He's close to sixty, dresses in a shirt with rolled-up sleeves worn over trousers, and is said to be more or less honest, although his personal honesty is somewhat tarnished because of various political compromises he's had to make. A pile of pipes will turn up where no tubewell is supposed to be; while a damaged school building awaits overdue repair, a hurriedly done road construction will swell the pockets of the contractor and the concerned department; Mahuldiha will be buzzing—with rumour, tension, dread; various broker groups will scramble for a share of the money scattered in Hari's name. Carried away by this expensive ceremony of a change of kings, the ordinary people will be distracted for a while; the people 80 percent of whom can't read, vote for a candidate only by recognizing the party symbol. It is to connect with them that the media engages in doing battle in all these forms and languages—wall writings, banners, posters, newspapers, electronic circuits. It amazes and saddens one to think of it.

Anyway, it's time to return home. The spirit of the Kanika bear must by now be on its way to heaven. I'm on the road to my residence after a tour through the city. Sanatan senses my troubled mood unerringly. On that day instead of taking the short cut, he takes me home after wandering a bit here and

there. The walled house is on the city's east end; marked by
a huge jaam tree. On summer days schoolchildren come to
gather the fallen fruit. The office is on one side, the 150 year-
old residence on the other, looking like a mysterious ancient
giant. In front of that, sitting on a string cot, Kuki is playing
with assorted brick and clay chips, all sorts of leaves and
bunches of grass. Nearby, Basumati is standing outside, the
light of the setting sun upon her body. As the car enters the
gate, crunching on the pebbled pathway, I see that I've two
strange visitors waiting for me. On the cemented seat under
the jaam tree is old Abinash-babu, Abinash Chakravarty, his
back resting against the tree trunk, his chin on his knees, his
stick laid next to him, a world of helplessness in his bifocal
glasses. And, how amazing, sitting crosslegged on the cot
before Kuki is that wonder boy—Bhajaman Juang. Aged
ten, in a wrinkled shirt and worn out half-pants, a faded
sack on one shoulder. He herds goats by day and studies at
night. Perhaps Kuki has had a bath again, I mean bathed
close to evening after a day of playing in dirt. Liberally oiled
before her bath, her hair, combed neatly, clings to her neck;
she is wearing Guddu's old singlet and briefs. With great
concentration she's putting grass and leaves in toy utensils
and handing them to Bhajaman, who equally attentively puts
them in his pocket—it's perhaps their shopkeeping game.
Seeing me, they all come running from different directions,
calling out in different ways. The game-playing, Abinash-
babu's dozing, Basumati's stance in the glow of the setting
sun—everything suddenly topsy-turvy.

I'm feeling truly happy to be back home; I'm sure the
mother bird, flying across the sky, flapping her tired wings
on her way back to the forest nest, is just this glad to see her
open-beaked nestlings. Kuki clings to my knees, smelling me.

My fingers are in her wet hair. The same fingers that signed
the death sentence for the poor bear this very morning.

5

In my dream I am under a bokul tree, lying on my back, my hands under my head. I see the tight weave of leaves above; I feel the free-flowing air on my eyelids, my face, my body; I sense I'm beside a river at sunrise. Yet I feel too lazy to even turn on my side. All around me is the fragrance of bokul flowers. Can one smell in a dream? Barely has this thought come when a metallic sound disturbs my sleep. Is it the alarm clock or is it someone turning the TV on? Pushing open heavy eyelids, I look at the telephone on the corner table. Yes, it's the phone ringing. The watch shows 5:15 in the afternoon; at first I thought it was morning. Outside the window, the birds are making a racket as they come in to roost among the trees. I realize I've been asleep. This is why I try not to put my head on a pillow after lunch. The accumulated weariness comes and sweeps over me. This is a Sunday. Perhaps that's why I fell asleep after eating, the mail edition of the newspaper still in my hands.

It's Guddu. He begins with a heart-breaking, 'O-o-o Ma!'

'What's the matter, love?'

'Today we've a practice on the sports ground and my socks are wet, my cap is wet. What am I going to wear?' His voice is choked with tears. It's not easy to solve this problem from this distance. I try, 'Will running a hot iron do? How wet are they?'

'Very. Both fell from the clothes-line into a tub of water.' Perhaps there's more to this than meets the eye. Could it be some sort of tussle with Ramprasad that led to this accident?

'You have a pair of brown socks. Wear those. And one day without the cap is all right.'

The cap is a recent addition. About three weeks ago, while giving him a haircut, our barber Raghu produced a military crew cut. I was in Swarupnagar that day, I'm the one who actually called him in from the playing field and sent him for a haircut. At first, Guddu didn't realize his hair had been cut so short, but the moment he was home, Rampasad gave it away by smirking. The problem was solved for the time being by buying him a cap. But now, wherever he goes, he must wear the cap, convinced that everyone is laughing at his closecut prickly hair. The trouble is, I'm the one who told him the story of a bear with bushy hair on his head and shaggy fur, who went to the monkey barber and came back with a shaved head—crying. The poor barber had fallen asleep while cutting his hair—he ran the scissors in his sleep, didn't even know. He ended up having to buy the bear a red turban in order to keep peace with him. 'Your Raghu-dada must have fallen asleep,' I wasn't sure whether or not to suppress a smile while comforting Guddu with the story.

Suddenly changing the topic, and cautiously lowering his voice, Guddu said, 'You know, Ma, yesterday when I was coming out of the school a man asked my name—'

'Haven't I told you not to talk to strangers?'

'I didn't tell him my name, Ma. But the man said he wasn't a stranger. He walked behind me for some time.'

'Who was with you?'

'Bultu was with me, and Ashok.'

'Have you told Baba?'

'I have. Baba said, "Hm," and if he comes again, I should ask him to come to our house. Baba asked me to tell you. The man has glasses, he's tall, the front of his head—'

'All right, I'm writing it down, you get a drawing of the man ready. Don't be afraid, all right? Don't go anywhere with him. If necessary, bring him home with you. Will you remember?'

Guddu seemed to be thinking a little, then he said, 'He isn't a kidnapper then?'

I smiled. 'No, not a kidnapper. But we've to handle him carefully, love.'

'Who's he?'

'When you've grown up a little, I'll explain to you.'

Just then, Ranjan came and took the telephone from Guddu: I could hear the sound of Guddu's feet as he ran off and I don't have the slightest inclination to write about the exchange I had with Ranjan. I kept thinking about how Guddu was growing up, unseen by me. How come he never asked, 'When are you coming, Ma?' when I called home. The last time he'd done so, it took me several days and nights to get over the pain of that question—it kept piercing me like a thorn for quite a while!

At the beginning of the month I had to go to Swarupnagar—I was going there after a gap of nearly a month and a half: the pressure of work was such that I hadn't been able to step outside of Mahuldiha. In Swarupnagar, I had two meetings on two consecutive days, in the home and revenue departments. After spending two days, I started off after dinner for Mahuldiha. As I headed north along

the national highway, it seemed as though I were leaving
for good. Pulling and tearing through the thousand vines
and tendrils entwined around my heart, I was going away.
The star-filled purple-black sky came down very close to
the moving Kaluaburhan hilltop. The waning moon hung
like a broken brass plate, insecurely. From the long line of
the forest of bamboo, teak and acacia on my left came the
grasping smell of night, as the heat of the day cooled off
and the forest grew restless with a wind. It was close to the
end of Bhadra. All day this rocky ground had burned, the
black granite rocks looking like wild buffaloes. The smell
of the yellow sunshine trapped in their hearts now mixed
with the smell of wild flowers and karanja plums. From the
high branches of the trees hung vines heavy with clusters of
white flowers, swaying like elephant trunks; a batch of the
endlessly shed brown saal leaves flying ahead on the tarred
road towards a bend. I reached the bend, as if blown by a
strong wind, and saw the road curve further and disappear
into the hazy moonlight. The car rushed on like a breaking
wave. I was going away. Yet, on my grass-green sari I could
still smell the faint scent of Guddu's hair oil. He'd put his
arms around me and rubbed his head against my chest, just
for a few seconds, and the scent of his hair oil stayed with
me. A long time ago, on the road travelling from Betoa to
Daltongunj in the sharp noontime sun, a butterfly flitting
ahead of the jeep landed for an instant on the windshield.
For a long time the yellow dust from its wings stayed smeared
on the transparent glass.

Guddu had come to the door to watch me leave, as he
did every time. A broken branch from the mango tree in
his hand, he was checking on the stuff being loaded in the
car. My black leather case lay in a corner of the verandah

and had Guddu not pointed it out, Sanatan might have forgotten it. The bundle of papers, the tiffin carrier, the house deity's seat, a large cleaver—because the Mahuldiha setup lacked one—the coconut grater from the kitchen, lemons and a guava sapling in plastic bags, Guddu fetched all these little things for Sanatan. When everything was in and the trunk was closed and locked with a sound of inevitable finality, he looked at me with his huge eyes and asked, waving his head of cropped hair, 'When are you going to come again?'

On the veranda covered in madhabi vines, I knelt before him so I could see the shadow of myself in his two eyes. 'If there's a meeting, the very next month.'

And if there's no meeting, then?'

'Then it'll take longer. I'm not sure yet how long it'll be.'

Coming closer, he put his arms round my neck, leaned on me and rocked himself like that for some time. Then he stood up straight and said without any emotion, 'I'll go there with you. Can I?'

So many times I've answered this question in so many ways, and yet, blocking out my own emotions as though this was going to be for the last time, I said, 'You know there's not even one good school there. We're trying to have one, it'll take upto next year to be ready.'

'That's okay, I'd rather go to a bad school. You can teach me at home in the evenings.'

Looking at the fading daylight, I then handed my child my verdict—as if in a trial. 'That just can't be, love!'

Hesitating, Sanatan mildly suggested, 'Ma, very soon it's going to be too late to start off. We've to reach Bamanghati before midnight. Otherwise, of course, spending tonight in Swarupnagar, tomorrow morning very early...'

Guddu clapped and jumped at that. 'That'll be great fun! Then Ma will sleep in the middle, I on one side of her and Kuki on the other.'

'Ah, Sanatan!' Annoyed, I frowned at him, 'What are you talking about? You know what that phone call was about. I must be there by ten in the morning tomorrow. Why're you leading a small child on for nothing?'

Guddu took a fistful of my sari out of his mouth, and moved away. On his put-out face suddenly came the language of the stars in a dark sky.

Just then Kuki, who had been peacefully asleep in her cot, began to cry. Basumati came out bouncing her, chanting snatches of nursery rhymes in unintelligible Mundari. As if in anticipation of her tears, my right breast had begun to tingle—an unmistakable signal. I quickly covered my milk-soaked blouse with the sari's free end, took Kuki from Basumati's arms and left the scene.

I could hear Basumati comforting Guddu, reasoning with him in her broken Hindi, as she put Kuki's clothes, water bottle, powder, towel and all the little things in the back seat. 'Don't cry, Guddu-babu, okay? The baby's still small, and it's mother's milk, you know, she has to go with mother.'

It was eight in the evening before we set off. Ranjan was still not home. Even though Ramprasad was there, I still didn't feel like leaving Guddu on his own. I telephoned Ranjan: 'Why Ranjan, you promised to come, you said you'd be back by seven.'

His mild voice and a slight laugh floated over the line, 'Why're you so worked up? Don't you ever get late yourself after making promises? I'm tied up here with something. Rather than worry, why don't you get started? I'll be back in ten minutes.'

Guddu took his mango branch and ran to the gate, opening it with great enthusiasm, saying, 'Ma, Ma, come again to our house, all right?'

As I turned the bend in the road, I looked back and saw him standing at the gate, the hair on his head cropped like a kadam flower, one hand in his pocket, the other holding that ubiquitous stick.

Alone.

Kuki's head was on my lap. Despite the half-open window, her back was soaked in sweat, also the back of her head, her overgrown hair. Her tiny, soft feet on the bag of clothes, the little girl was sound asleep. It seemed like it was only the other day that Guddu had been like this. I remember, walking in the afternoon with him in my arms, his drool wetting my shoulder. A bird called out 'ku-u ku-u' from behind the foliage, and immediately Guddu would lift his face from my shoulder, as though it was somewhere very close, and he expected it to fly in and sit by him on my shoulder. It was just the other day. Seems like yesterday, when I was slowly waking from the mist of anasthesia one dawn of Paush, my limbs feeling as though still under water, only the face seeming to float on the surface. The painful bite of the drip needle on the back of the hand, a throbbing pain inside my head. Pushing my heavy eyelids open, I asked, even in the midst of this, 'He…where is he?'

Not Guddu, how strange, but Ranjan, I was then like a drowning person looking just for Ranjan. People from my family and Ranjan's thought I was asking to see the newborn, as all new mothers do immediately they open their eyes. Someone, I don't recall who, held him up and showed him to me, 'Look, you've a boy. No defect, after all, a perfect wax doll.'

That's when I first met Swapno. Yes, he was named Swapno. That unreal baby lay in a green slip like a bunch of pink flowers; perfect lips, thin and red, his long lashes over closed eyelids, and such a big nose! Why? I lifted a hand with difficulty and touched his fist, closed tight like a conch. Then, before the flood of sleep carried me away, I called Ranjan's name one last time.

Let Ranjan come and cut me off the umbilical cord of the past and deliver me in the lap of present and future.

How the days raced past like a gust of wind. Guddu or Swapno grew up in the blink of an eye. The one that stood by the gate, alone, uncomprehending—is he that wax doll?

At this moment, I can still feel his arms around my neck, the milky smell of his body very close to my nose, I'm trying with all my strength to ease myself out of his arms, but I can't. At the same time, flying away so quickly like a tawny leaf of Chaitra, I keep saying, 'Guddu, I'm so far away from you!'

Quickly glancing at the mirror with anxious eyes, Sanatan saw me, saw the tears rolling down from under my tinted glasses, and he slowed the car and moved it to one side of the road, but he didn't stop the engine, because he knew I must reach Bamanghati before midnight.

Basumati was looking at me with a mix of anxiety and anguish. A few gray-black strands of her curly hair in front were shivering slightly. She would have felt better if she could distract me the way she could a baby. Since that was not possible, she placed her rough hand gently on mine. When I watch the creases on Basumati's prematurely aged face, the brass flower on her pierced nose, her tattooed cheeks, I think of Dhanai. Dhanai or Dhanajay, who went to see the fair at the Relegada ground, and never came back. Worn out from the endless complicated labyrinthine process of searching, an old and awkward Basumati finally came to me asking for a job. That was the first time, and the only time, I heard her mention Dhanai. Once she took Kuki in her arms, she didn't ever speak his name again. When we go to the Swarupnagar house, Basumati plays very enthusiastically with Guddu as well. I know she gets someone or the other to read to her from old newspapers, because she can't read herself, in case Dhanai's name somehow springs out from all the other news.

Even in all her suffering and indigence, Basumati hadn't lost the heart to give me comfort.

We were again travelling fast towards Bamanghati. I had lowered the windows, so Kuki wouldn't be hot. If she's hot, she turns from side to side, cries and then, what's most dangerous, wakes up and starts moving around. I know, though I can't actually see, that the pupils under her dream-soaked closed eyelids are moving about a little at a time. Gently wiping the sweat off her neck with a hand towel, I watch her little body rise and fall as she breathes. Once in a while as though obeying some mantra, she sinks into the depths of sleep, before resuming the normal rhythm of her breathing.

The wind rushes in from all sides. From the creases in the road, dust rises and settles into my hair, and with that, all sorts of smells of joys and sorrows mix in my consciousness—smells of burnt bidis, green saal leaves, discarded burnt clay pots. Once the eyes get accustomed to staring at darkness, various stories about those who live in darkness swim up to the mind's surface. In the village below the hill outlined against the sky, the inhabitants eat their meagre supper in darkness, they drink fermented mahul, and then, with their entire bodies gripped by exhaustion, they stretch out on a mat and fall asleep. The sleeping child's feet up on the mother's body, the labourer woman's head on her husband's arm. Crickets move with a dry rustle through the straw bed. And amidst this, the old couple snoring loudly like the sound from a cracked conch shell. Saving the last two ounces of kerosene for cooking the next supper, they go to sleep early. There's no electricity—not in the homes, not on the street, there's no oil, candles cost too much, no wood to be had, the forest has receded like the sea at low tide, what can they do except sleep?

The other day in the air-conditioned seminar hall, Alan Ford the American demographer, flung at his audience the ultimate theory, sharp as the edge of a palm leaf—pill, motivation, these things are no good, your population problem is basically that of darkness. There's no light, nothing else can be done, so—copulate, multiply—that's all. Give them light bulbs, give them TVs, give them videos, you'll see the rate of population growth will automatically go down. I started to say something, just as Rohit Bhatia, sitting next to me, came out with 'hear hear!' but my friend Arindam Sen lightly touched my arm—'Arre, arre, hang on, has he come here to listen to you?'

'Does that mean he can say anything, without a sense of reality, sitting in an air-conditioned office, thinking he knows everything about the country?'

'Ah, you're incorrigible!' With that, Arindam leaned back in his chair.

Bamanghati, shortly after midnight. That night I did not sleep. Looking at the still ocean of the freshly made white bed, I thought about Guddu. The sight of this kind of bed always starts a bug of mischief in his head. 'I'm swimming, look, Ma, I'm swimming,' and in a second, wildly jumping, thrashing, somersaulting, he makes a mess of such a smooth vision of peace. Of course, I knew that, at this very moment he was asleep, the mosquito net puffing out with the breeze generated by the electric fan, the pale moonlight through the window on his forehead or cheek, his lips slightly parted, perhaps he's rapidly sinking into pure dream. Until a few years ago, turning in his sleep, Guddu would brush his hand across the sheet as if looking for someone. These days, that search has ceased, without his being conscious that it has. He has come to sense that, in darkness a boat moves on alone pulled by the water's current, swaying uncertainly just like this.

Five hundred and fifty kilometres. Ten hours of crossing forests, outposts, hills and valleys. Between Swarupnagar and Mahuldiha. The measure of my distance from Swapno and Ranjan. Whenever I mentioned this distance, Ranjan would remark in his mild, oblique manner, 'There are ways for one who wants to reduce the distance, not for one who wants to increase it.' The other day when Guddu called, this is what he said again. I said nothing in reply. I was more worried about the context in which Ranjan said it. I was so far from them, that it's out of the question to be with them if it becomes necessary to be together for some time.

'I thought, this time you went to Calcutta, you settled everything,' Ranjan said.

'I also thought so, Ranjan, but now I see the matter isn't settled at all.'

Somnath came to Guddu's school. How strange! What does he want? To this day, I haven't been able to figure out the way his mind works. The memory of that nine-and-a-half-year-old- scene no longer brings tears to my eyes, it's just a bitter thought inside my head. It doesn't hurt. As though that wound has grown hard, with no sensation left.

It's drizzling. A Bengali girl is running along the crowded streets of Old Delhi. She's wearing an expensive silk sari, a vermilion dot on her forehead, light lipstick, but more than her makeup or clothes, what's visible on her face, in her eyes, is—an acute fear. On the streets of Daryaganj, the afternoon sidewalk-bazaar is overflowing—fruit shops, cut-piece shops, motor parts, Bengali sweets. Babli keeps running. She doesn't know in which direction, but she knows it's the direction that's away from danger. In her handbag there's just twenty-two rupees and some change. A doctor by the name of Alak Mitra lives in Sarojini Nagar, his address is written on a slip of paper in her handbag. He's the younger brother of a professor of her elder brother. Is the address still valid? She got it four or five years ago, when they'd first come to Delhi on a trip. Suppose the address has changed? The girl isn't thinking anything at all, her mind is without sensation, her head feels light and yet inside it seems filled with smoke like that of the Kanika forest bear on the run. For now, she's just running away. In an almost supernatural coincidence, an elderly Sikh gentleman offers to give her a ride on his scooter and drop her off at Sarojini Nagar. Neither Alak Mitra nor his wife had met her earlier, at first they were confounded. They had no idea how long her domestic crisis would last, or how many days she was going to stay in their house, and yet Mrs. Mitra wiped her face with a wet towel with such tenderness and helped her to change her clothes. Perhaps she realized, but in that hazy situation, even bending over the bathroom basin, Babli didn't realize that Swapno had arrived. That she wasn't alone any more; from now on that unreal baby was to stay with her, even on the twisted road of her escape.

Somnath, his parents, his elder sister—it was impossible for Babli to understand their psychology. Somnath was crazy about marrying her; there was a time when he waited for hours at the head of the lane where Babli lived with her family, or by the gate of her office. Lost in the five-o'clock crowd in the lift, she'd step out and there Somnath would be, before her, in dark glasses, almost six feet tall, the hair in front of his head not thinning as yet, a briefcase in his hand.

That time was one of considerable stress and anguish for Babli. Nothing there seemed to agree with her. She couldn't put her mind to anything. The constant thought in her mind was: if only she could break off all ties and go somewhere far away. The ugly environment at the office, with piles of dusty files crowding from all sides, the venereal-diseased, prematurely-aged Samanta's table-thumping toothless laughter, Rabi-da's constant scratching under his kurta, Shibesh Burman's scoldings, the vapour and odour from the drain below, the corridors with their pungent smell of mudi and onions—the combination of all this pushed Babli to the edge of a pit. Jump a little and there's bottomless darkness. Somnath was the only hint of escape from that darkness. 'Delhi, I'm going to Delhi,' as though once in Delhi, she'd have in her hands a kind of all-India warranty of freedom.

'I'm going to Delhi,' she said with mild pride, putting the resignation letter on Shibesh Burman's desk.

Did Shibesh regard her unscathed escape from the grindstone with sadness tinged with a bit of jealousy? He said, 'That's nice, much better opportunities there, and you've a bright career, maybe one day after taking the competitive exams—'

'You'll land the post of our boss,' the new section officer Amiya at the next desk smiled with self-satisfaction.

In those days spent in an uncontrollable desire to escape, her only consolation was the poetry tabloid printed at their own expense with Tapan, a junior assistant from the irrigation department, Jyotirmoy of the library and Prahlad Jana of the relief department, who'd recently been transferred from Medinipur. It was a joy to sit with them in the canteen exchanging poems. Prahlad walked to save bus fare, from the office in Dalhousie Square to Sealdah, to tutor a schoolgirl, then to his boarding house in Moulali. Jyotirmoy had two ever-hungry mouths to feed at home and there was his paralysed father. Tapan's family was relatively affluent, with paddyland and a house in Bardhaman; except for his elder sister who had been sent back by her in-laws. They all loved poetry, and hadn't stopped writing it through their ups and downs. The day their paper came out, the four of them celebrated by sharing a chicken omelet cut into four.

Prahlad, Jyotirmoy and the others were sorry to hear of Babli's leaving and seeking escape through marriage. But they didn't say anything. On the contrary, together they bought a basketful of samosas and amartis from the sweet shop outside the office, and tea from the vendor in the corridor and treated everyone in the department. Babli had enough money with her, but they would not listen to her and so the four of them pooled together to pay the bill. Babli didn't quite notice the glint of sadness in Prahlad's eyes. She was dreaming of the bit of blue sky glimpsed through the cell's bars.

⟨◈⟩

The day I went away was strangely clouded, sad. The train seemed like a tired yoked buffalo, blankly staring and waiting for the journey to start. Terribly muggy, it seemed like it was going to rain again like that morning. We had new suitcases, I wore a new sari, carried a vanity case. The moment the train moved, I would wipe off all the writing on the slate, making it clean and new. After the third whistle, my mother placed a hand at the train window where I sat and said, 'You're going in the month of Bhadra. All right, go.' Our family had never practised saying the customary 'come' for 'go'.

There are so many different kinds of people in this world. Even mental cruelty has been perfected into an art form through persistent honing. Village women show me the marks on their backs, marks that will probably go away with medication one day. But the sorrows etched on the mind's soapstone linger on. There are third-degree methods that leave no visible mark on the body, but make the insides bleed. Somnath was gradually trying that kind of method on me.

After just a month or two I realized that when leaving for office, he locked the place from outside. After returning, knowing I was locked in, he carried out a minute search of every corner, every window. The locking had to stop when his family came to visit from Calcutta: his retired father, inert, speechless, his mother and his elder sister. I was not allowed to go into the kitchen. I hadn't been allowed out alone anyway. What can it be called? Not dowry-related torture. He and his family had never raised any question of money, jewellery, demands for a refrigerator or TV, neither before the wedding, nor after. Later I learnt that his mother never wanted him to marry. I hadn't known much about Somnath's childhood at the time. It didn't seem believable to me that three consecutive attacks of typhoid could turn someone into a malicious, angry, and cruel person. Perhaps all this had remained hidden, dormant in his very blood. The boy and his elder sister would take a mouse out of the trap and watch while hot water was poured on it; many years later they would push an unrelated lone girl away from home with innovative methods of torture. They would get hold of weird clothes and demand that I put them on. Or they'd ask me to wear a thick layer of lipstick in the afternoon heat. They'd drink alcohol after dinner, and demand that I sit in a chair before them or join them in drinking. Or they would put on a record and insist that I dance, and enlarged photographs of that forced dance would be put up on the drawing room wall. My letters to my family could be mailed only after they had read them. I felt myself shrivelling up. It was at this time that, one day, the cage suddenly opened.

In a rare moment of softness, Somnath was taking me out for a good Bengali movie. I dressed with care, in a silk sari, and light jewellery. Very carefully I hid my agitation and fear, and told my mother-in-law that I would clean the floors after coming back. (Oh yes, the first thing she did after I came into the family was to get rid of the part-time maid, claiming that maids were gossip-mongers!) Then, as soon as Somnath's back was turned as he queued up for tickets I stepped away and started running. That was the end of Somnath! Nine years later, after I came to Mahuldiha, I got the first of his letters.

"Babli, come back. I can't live without you. I made mistakes, of course, but I made mistakes because I loved you. Do you know, all this time I haven't been able to look at any other girl? It's been three years since I came back to Calcutta. I heard you named the boy Swapno. I long to see him. Will you let me see him? Who does he look like, you or me? Blahblahblah." Three or four pages filled out in small handwriting. I was fearful at first. Luckily, I had mastered the skill of hiding fear. What if he turned up? Swapno knew nothing at all. Not yet. He's not old enough to understand. When he is, Ranjan and I will explain to him. I showed the letter to Ranjan.

There was no trouble in getting the divorce. But in the interim for a whole year I felt I was walking on thorns. Ranjan was with me, or else I would've just given up. Ranjan separated me from my past, cutting the cord with the sharp knife of his sensibility. Otherwise, how could I have imagined that with Swapno in my arms and my mind so wounded, I would plunge into the all-India competitive exams to fulfil Shibesh Burman's prediction?

Somnath wrote several more letters. I learned that he came to Mahuldiha and looked around, though confronting me was not his goal. He was looking for Swapno. We decided, and 80 percent of this decision was Ranjan's advice, to keep all the doors wide open for this woodworm called Somnath. We loathed him, we did not fear him—it was important he knew this. Finding all avenues closed would only induce him to change tactics, this much I knew. Once, I tried to talk to him directly, several months ago when I was in Calcutta. I looked up his telephone number and called from a public telephone. He was surprised. 'Babli, where are you calling from?'

'Somnath, what do you want? Money? Some other kind of settlement?'

'Babli, I want to see you once,' he said.

'You can come and see me any time you like in Mahuldiha or in Swarupnagar, but not in Calcutta,' I said.

After a moment's silence, his curiosity got the better of him, 'Do the people in Mahuldiha know?'

'About my past? No, we're all waiting for when you'll come and stick posters on the walls.'

'Babli, do you think I'm so mean?' His voice now had a touch of sadness.

'I don't think anything of you, Somnath. The reason I called is just to let you know this—if you try to harm Swapno in any way physically or mentally, then you'll regret it all your life.'

Somnath, of course, gave no importance to my warning. Because, he came to Swarupnagar after that, and to Mahuldiha. One day in the bathroom at Swarupnagar, I was drying Kuki with a towel after bathing her, when suddenly I looked through the glass window and noticed him outside. Somnath standing under the flowering radhachurha tree across the road. Eyes covered with dark glasses, tall, balding in front, one hand in his pocket, as though he was suddenly going to pull out a gun! I sent Ramprasad— go, ask that man to come inside. As soon as Ramprasad drew near, Somnath quickly walked off. Coward. Greedy. Weak. Almost like an insect that you don't want to touch even to kill it.

Right now, when I'm so far away from Guddu, I need Ranjan's support badly. I know Ranjan stands by me, yet his quiet indifference, or his cutting humour, on the telephone or in the brief periods when I see him in Swarupnagar, pierces me, hurts me. Why does Ranjan act this way? Why won't he talk to me about this on his own initiative, why won't he let me know that he's always with me, that he would never leave me?

My own of ego has come to stand between us. I have never said openly to him, 'Please, Ranjan, make sure that Somnath doesn't tear Swapno away from us.' No, not physically tear away. Somnath doesn't have the willpower for that, nor is it his goal. What I'm apprehensive of is that Swapno, who doesn't know anything of his past, would hear about it the first time in his life from that depraved, twisted man. To defeat this innocent-seeming attempt at blackmail, what is needed is courage, a lot of courage. Somnath doesn't want to fight a direct battle, the hand of law can't touch him, his letters do not mention blackmail. In the eyes of society, he's just a memory-haunted, lonely ex-husband, ex-lover. Anyone who knows well knows that Somnath has just two goals. To throw a large rock in the village pond that's Mahuldiha and disappear from the scene. And to fill a child's ears with stories that will instantly pull the ground from under his feet. Just this. That is exactly why it's impossible to fight Somnath without being totally unarmed and totally fearless. Ranjan knows this. Ranjan knows my mind very well indeed.

This young man's mild yet firm personality, his razor-sharp steely sarcasm, his polished unemotional behaviour—none of this is unknown to me. It was for exactly this combination that I once loved Ranjan. Why use the past tense, I still do! In spite of everything Ranjan Srivastava made Swapno and me his own, pushing aside my marked past as something insignificant. His own people's customs, traditions, hopes and expectations, nothing deterred him from doing as he wanted. In the last nine years Ranjan has not changed, only a wall of coldness has descended between us—from about two years ago. The incident was actually quite trivial, at least I could have taken it lightly if I wanted to. The trouble is my nature, my strangely wilful nature. At a time when I should have claimed what life offered me, I left empty-handed without so much as a word. And yet, my mind started getting in battle mode over a minor accounting discrepancy.

That was the first, and perhaps the last time that I broke the code of our everyday life and asked Ranjan to explain a period of absence. Ranjan looked at me sternly and said in his usual mild voice, 'I'm not telling. I don't take tests in trustworthiness.' From that moment on he cut himself off from me and moved behind a wall of ice. Since then, although we live together in the same house, sleep in the same bed, neither of us can reach out to the other with a hand and touch. Neither can hear the other's real voice. As though Ranjan and I have left our bodies of flesh and blood and turned into black-and-white pictures. We sit down to eat and he appreciates my cooking; on the way back from Delhi he buys toys and clothes for Swapno and Kuki; I put ironed handkerchiefs in his pocket when I find time, buy a birthday present and leave it under his pillow. The rhythm is not broken anywhere, yet the soul of the poem, as it were, has left its body.

Not that I haven't judged and found myself lacking. It was just a name and telephone number. In the kind life we live, who has the time to get worked up and suspicious over such minor questions? Especially for us, whose daily work, mornings and afternoons, involves dealing with countless faces and names. Still, a part of my mind turned stubborn and kept insisting on wanting to know. If it's so insignificant, then why won't Ranjan tell me who she is? Have I not yet earned the right to share something more than a curt 'It's not possible to tell you now'? At that time I lived in Swarupnagar; it was much later that I moved alone to Mahuldiha. On the first page of the blue telephone diary, a new number had been added near the bottom. In pencil in Ranjan's handwriting: seven eight two nine zero, Uttara. Ranjan could have written it under U. Why write it on the first page? 'Because I need it often, it's inconvenient if I've to search for it each time.' Very brief answer.

Before Kuki's birth, I was physically unwell. My feet had swollen up because of high blood pressure. I had just started my leave, rather late, as it hadn't been possible to get time off earlier. According to calculations, Kuki was not due for two more weeks. Around eight in the evening, my body seemed to be giving way, twisted with pain. So soon? My feet were cold, growing numb, and labour pains started wringing the lower abdomen. Swapno was just about to sit down to eat, Ranjan wasn't back from office yet, I had just sent Ramprasad to the market for something and he was later than he should have been. I was frightened. The memory of Swapno's difficult birth filled me with dread. I needed Ranjan then, I needed him badly. Just then the phone rang. A woman's voice, she too was trying to get in touch with Ranjan.

'Ranjan isn't home, he may still be at the office, he isn't back yet.'

'Please give me the office telephone number.'

I gave it and asked for hers. 'Seven eight two nine zero. Please, give a message to Ranjan, in case I don't reach him at the office.'

'Go ahead.'

'Tell him that Uttara is waiting for him,' said the sad-sounding elderly female voice and then she rang off.

In the clutch of fear, anxiety and exhaustion, I hurried Swapno through the meal by feeding him. Getting him washed took another fifteen minutes. Then I called the office, but I couldn't reach Ranjan. And Ranjan didn't come home either. It was nine in the evening, ten. Then, eleven. Anxious Ramprasad was at a loss about what to do.

The doctor was someone we knew well. I called a taxi and got to the hospital around eleven-thirty. Ramprasad was to stay with the sleeping Swapno. But what would happen when he woke up the next morning? What if Ranjan was still not back? What would Guddu do? At five in the morning, before the glow of sunrise came on the sky's forehead, I heard Kuki's cry. For the last five hours of my labour I'd been caught in the grip of fear, anxiety, suspicion, hurt, everything, and now deep sleep was enveloping my body. The doctor, who'd been up all night, was preparing to go home. Apart from the nurse in the room, I was alone. Without a relative or a friend, completely alone. More than anything else, I felt the embarrassment of Ranjan's absence. This was the same Ranjan who had stood by his girlfriend (before he married me) when she had a child nine years ago. Now he couldn't even get back home from office in time for the birth of his own first child. Not even a call, no message. The doctor was, of course, feeling awkward that I was alone, though he couldn't say anything. Amidst the chaos of a government hospital, he had to run around himself to do the necessary preparations. The nurse's look held a kind of unspoken pity. What must they be thinking of me?

The voice that said 'Uttara is waiting' kept piercing through me even as I slept.

Ranjan came at nine in the morning. Clearly, he had had a bath, his clothes were fresh. Leaning over, he looked at Kuki, the sleeping Kuki. Then he smiled at me soothingly and said, 'Suffered a lot, haven't you? I couldn't come, last night I was in a place—'

'Uttara was waiting?' Without trying to hide my annoyance, I meant to give him back the heap of ignominy that landed on me. Took him the whole night to come to the hospital? For the first time I hurled an adjective at him: 'Irresponsible!'

Glancing back and forth between Swapno standing by the door and me, Ranjan said briefly, 'Babli, it's not possible to tell you now, not in this condition.'

I said, 'I'll never want to know, even if it kills me, I hope you'll remember that.'

'It's better not to swear in the heat of the moment. Once out, words can't be taken back,' he said in a resigned tone.

'But I don't, I don't want to take them back.' In front of the confused Swapno I buried my face in the pillow and sobbed.

Ranjan didn't want to wait. Taking Swapno's hand, he went back home in his silent reserve.

Once again, I was alone with Kuki.

Even the curtain of chill could have lifted, had I not left for Mahuldiha. Five hundred and fifty kilometres away. There was no adequate school for Swapno, and the hospital cold storage didn't work because of electricity shortages.

'I don't want to influence you,' Ranjan said, 'But if you don't want to go, they won't force you. It is up to you to think and decide.'

I came away. With six-month old Kuki, her playthings, clothes and bedding, my books and papers, a little furniture and just two suitcases. I came here one hectic day, to this land of mahua trees. I had to leave my treasured Swapno behind in Swarupnagar with Ranjan, to avoid his having to change school in mid-session, but still I didn't appeal to the authorities for consideration. I didn't beg them to reconsider the order and let me stay with my family.

In this one decade that has passed since Babli left Somnath and his family at Daryaganj, she has not begged anyone for kind consideration. Time has taught her to throw aside the feather-light crown of love's warm company for the sharp sword of self-respect.

6

Bhajaman Juang comes out of the back door, contentedly wiping his hand on his half-pants. Clearly, Basumati has fed him a stomachful.

'Where are you going this late? Stay the night here.'

The boy smiles, shaking his head to say no.

Basumati says that Bharat, Anadi and others from his village are at the bus depot, they came to the godown with their collections of kendu leaves. If he starts out now, they'd all be in Kusumpota together by the last bus.

As he leaves, Bhajaman throws a question at me, 'Will you take me to Calcutta when I finish the *Tritiya Bhag* (third-level primer)?'

'Finish it first!'

'I'm up to "Manohar's Rates of Interest". Fifteen more days and the book will be finished. After that, you've got to!'

As I watch him leave, I feel a sort of ache in my heart. Then I realize it's not pain, but something much stronger, much bigger—the feeling that comes when sadness mixes with pride and a sense of triumph, the kind of storm that rises inside when watching a mere mortal reaching for the sky. Can he do it? This boy who is the same age as my Swapno!

An orphan, he lives in a crumbling mud hut with his uncle and aunt. During the day, he takes his uncle Shibram Juang's goats out to graze. He collects mahua, picks kendu leaves, or fills baskets with saal seeds, depending on the season. In Kusumpota mouza of villages there's only one primary school, run by the Juang Unnayan Project field office. Bhajaman does not attend that school. During school hours, the boy is extremely busy elsewhere, all day he has to go around gleaning bits and pieces for survival. He gets up at dawn, goes out on a bowl of mandia gruel, gets no other food till evening, except for the occasional fruit or whatever he may find in the forest. About a month ago, when I was walking the stony arid paths of Kusumpota, something suddenly caught my attention near a fenced yard. It was a summer evening. The sky held some faint light, not turning dark all at once as on winter evenings.

I heard a sort of buzz—a noise that sounded like people studying together. It was the same line that they were reading aloud, but their pronunciations and manner of reading were all so different that the result was like a haphazard assortment of sounds. I simply had to go in and look. Sitting before two sooty lanterns and bending over torn copies of a primer, some twenty or twenty-two young and middle-aged men and women were doing battle the with the letters of the alphabet. Apparently, old primers, broken slates etc., had come from the school. The teacher was the widowed mother of a worker of Kusumpota anganwadi, she ran off to hide but was stopped. They come to study at duskfall, I was told. They'd keep nodding off because they were so tired from the day's work, yet they won't leave, and moreover, keep asking the teacher, 'Don't you know English? We want to learn English.'

'Read me a little, let me see how well you've learnt', I said.

They looked at each other's faces, bare-chested men in short dhotis, dry-haired women in cheap mill saris; some picked at their nails with embarrassment, some rubbed one foot against the other; some took deep breaths in panic, chests working like bellows. Clearly, in learning abilities they were all Ma Saraswatis. They all read aloud together because the pages were more or less memorised because they'd been repeated so often, but reading out one at a time felt too scary, because the letters started dancing before the eyes like so many big black ants.

From this bunch quickly stepped out that wonder boy—Bhajaman Juang.

'Arre, this small boy, what is he doing here? Ei, don't you go to the school?'

'How can I go to the school, it's held during the day. I herd the goats then.'

Taking up a book, Bhajaman began to read fluently. In just a month and a half he had learnt to read his torn copy in its entirety. He had learnt writing before any of them, and most important, learnt arithmetic.

He didn't seem intimidated, like some gaping village herdboy, before people like us from outside; he wanted to come to Mahuldiha with me, he wanted to know too when exactly the circus would be visiting in winter. Since then they've been sent new copies of first, second and third primers for functional literacy, they've got slates and chalk; and they've started a cooperative fund to buy kerosene. The panchayat is also giving prizes to good students. Evening classes have begun in hundreds of villages like Kusumpota, which feels proud at having been the first! And Bhajaman Juang is the first one from this area to have done well. From a pupil, he has now been promoted to a teacher—because Shanti the teacher can no longer manage the whole class by herself.

Bhajaman has not yet seen the circus, though. But, he has already visited Mahuldiha three times. Walking in through that iron gate with complete ease, he has told me about their various needs and complaints. About the market being out of kerosene. About the school's teacher often being absent, the students having to go back day after day. About the anganwadi almost running out of the powdered cereal they provide. As though he was Kusumpota's designated spokesman. Bhajaman now wants to go, beyond Mahuldiha, to see the country. This time, as soon as the third primer is finished, he's going to go to Calcutta. The future lies before him like a dark cave, no light in his home, no food, having to fast for days if the monsoon does not come on time. Where will Bhajaman head after the third primer? It may be possible to push for his admission in the fifth grade, but will he be able to finish school? Will he ever become a college graduate and get within jumping reach of the office position reserved for him? Will he ever be able to find his way through assorted mazes and snatch a cooperative loan for himself?

In 1856, the anthropologist E. A. Samuel found some of these people clothed in just two leafy branches. Later, in 1931 they were rediscovered by Vivian Mick; they were still dressed in the same way. The Juangs live like stone-age people, Mick wrote, on fruit from the forest and roots dug up from the ground. As early as 1940 Verrier Elwin saw them doing jhum cultivation, which shows the Juangs to be much more advanced than in Mick's observation. Apparently, they didn't scatter the seeds on the ashes of burnt wild growth; instead, they made little holes in the earth with small iron plough-heads and put the seeds in. In the last thirty years, jhum cultivation has shrunk. The forests on the steeper hills are watched by forest guards. The forests burnt in the last decade haven't had much chance to grow back—the shortage of land makes the farmers return to burn them in three or four years, and they are driven back by the guards. Finally, the (Juang Unnayan) Project and the forest department have reached a compromise to give them some land on the plains. They've been given demonstrations a few times on how to raise paddy, potatoes, groundnuts and oilseeds. But how many of them can really turn out a living that way?

This densely forested valley, through which cricket calls ring even during the day, is surrounded by impassable hills. Somewhere in there is hidden the source of an underground river, seen flowing in a rill out of a pond, then getting lost, and reappearing a mile and a half west amidst deep forest. The story goes that a long time ago a virtuous Juang brought this river in here, that's why the Juangs call themselves children of the sage. Numbering close to 45,000, they live scattered all over this valley. I was startled to see the statistics on record. The literacy rate is only 8 percent for males, not even 1 percent for females; child mortality is close to 160 per thousand. Being one of the more inaccessible areas of the world has of course been a blessing in disguise in some ways. Sawmill owners, armed with logging licenses, haven't as yet started their onslaught; nor are bands of contractors setting up camps to take away the bamboo forests. However, the opposite has also happened. Wherever the hillside is cut to build a road, the first to rush in are the trucks of wholesalers, and tractors rented by moneylenders, and with them come gambling and liquor. But there are no roads in the remote corners of this frontier. So news of deaths from cholera or enteric fever doesn't easily reach the outside world. An adolescent mother giving birth to twins has died in agony, the babies' bodies only partially out of hers. The night dark, no road, no vehicle, and hardly anyone there to take her to a hospital. The project's field staff sit around sucking their thumbs and, lamenting that ten years have passed and still these people have not been civilized. Out of every ten people asked to come for training, they say, only two or three turn up. Even if you desperately try showing them new methods of cultivation, they won't try those out. Absolute savages, these people. In these ten years have these babus understood even an iota of the Juangs' lifestyle, their intimate relationship with the forest, their customs and codes of conduct, their social ties? Do they expect these people to flock to them like birds if they just cast a few crumbs in their direction?

'How do you feel today, Dhwantari?' Sitting in the porch of his home, Dhwantari smiles his toothless smile in response, and continues to look at the ground. A major wave of cerebral malaria has swept over this area. Though it took many lives— of children, adolescents, newly-married youths—Dhwantari is still alive. Even like this, just sitting in the autumn sun, he is often shaken by the fever. A load of crinkly white hair on his head, his age beyond count, he's like the trees and rocks. Sometime ago, in explaining the complex social rules of their community and the dynamics of clan structure to me, Dhwantari pointed his finger to the forest and said, "It's there, eleven brothers went over there to farm. Before clearing the forest to prepare the land, each one marked a tree with his axe; that's how Dharamdeo came; the forest around a tree became a seat, a throne; from each seat later emerged a clan." Dhwantari said that for them the village was one family; that's why there could be no marriage between men and women of the same village, wives must come from other villages. Dharamdeo is believed to have created this earth, these hills, the river underground, these trees. Yet there's no image of Dharamdeo anywhere, no temple. Of course the village goddess is worshipped in a stone and anointed with oil and vermilion. But Dharamdeo is never revealed to human eyes. Perhaps very late at night, when moonlight on the hilltop mixes with the smell of saal flowers, when light and shadow play on the dew-damp ground like the original man and woman in coitus, then this non-manifest deity walks silently across the valley, from village to village. At the musky scent from the deity's body, the ruthless leopard wakes up and licks its paws and baby elephants on the Narayan hill are startled by the deity visiting their dreams.

Everyone still believes in what Dhwantari says, even though he doesn't talk much these days. Even the project's Nitai-babu has to find ways to tap Dhwantari's influence when he's in a fix. Opening his swollen, heavy eyelids with difficulty, he looks at me. He smiles again. As feet walk the ground in front of his downcast eyes—he knows them by sight—a child's muddy titlark feet, a young woman's anklet-clad feet, a young man's dry cracked feet in rubber sandals. He continues to look down as if eager to study the border of my handloom sari. But suddenly, in the heat of the sun, the yellow of mustard flowers seems to fill his eyes. And, exhausted, he falls asleep again, squatting there, his head tucked between his knees.

Dhwantari, however, has accomplished a major task. He was given a book to look at—titled 'Know about Life'. It had a green cover and was freshly printed. I watched him as he felt the book, smelt it, turned it around. Then he smiled and said, 'let the men and the women read it.' He'd watch them sitting right here, on this porch.

Who lit the first lamp? No one remembers this any longer. Now, not just in Kusumpota, but throughout the district—in the nooks and crannies of Mahuldiha, a thousand clay lamps are glimmering. Before the first one was lit, however, many days and many nights were spent in the task of preparing the wicks. Ranadeb Chaudhuri, besieged by doubts and apprehensions, sent his paid goondas everywhere to find out what was going on. What were they up to? The frequent meetings, rallies, marches, torch-flame processions—was all this non-political? How could that ever be? Must be that bastard Bikram Sardar making his political profit out of it, go find out! Bikram Sardar, being an intelligent political entrepreneur, anticipated the problem and begged, 'Please don't ask me to join you, I beg you with folded hands, I don't want to get involved in these things.' But, others gradually came forward to join: volunteer organizations like Banabasi Sangha, Adivasi Mukti Bahini, even the elected panchayat members, Teachers' Federation workers. In distant villages with no more than one or two educated women, the anganwadi workers and the healthcare staff have come forward. Day in and day out the wall writing went on by twilight and at dawn. The elderly Sarvodaya leader Avinash-babu mobilized neighbourhood boys to make the posters.

Initially the Kumardihi cultural society did some street plays. They came by bus at their own expense and gave performances at two or three of the panchayats. Then one day the young boys and girls of the local clubs Bichitra and Bokultala came up and demanded: 'What's this? Don't the youth of Mahuldiha have any artistic talent? Why do performers have to be called in from outside? We're writing new plays.' Hundreds of plays, yatras, skits were written in the next few months. The message was, after all, staring us in the face. Know the world. Figure out the accounts that affect you, you're surrounded by the mahajans, the traders, the bank babus, the officials. If you must pay good money to brokers just to have a printed paper read out to you or a form filled out for you, then how are you going to fight? How much longer are you going to live the lives of bonded labourers and ploughmen? Come on, take up the pen first.

Abinash-babu, our Sarvodayee, and Akhil-babu, the elderly leader of the Teachers' Federation, came within an inch of hand-to-hand combat. When Abinash-babu in his quiet, calm and grave tone said: 'In village after village, everywhere, we're confronted with this question, in the last forty years have the teachers done what they were supposed to? Over 40 percent of teachers in this district do not attend schools regularly. In 30 percent of primary schools the teacher on the job does not stay in the village. He commutes; he never arrives before ten and by two-thirty he's ready to leave. Today, if teachers want to take a leadership role in the training of literacy workers, that's well and good, but the people are bound to ask: What were you doing all this time? Today's adult illiterates are the school- missed, dropout and never-schooled children of the post-independence years.'

Akhil-babu, a roundish man, short in height, with a shiny bald head, in a homespun kurta with rolled sleeves over a dhoti, and always with high blood pressure, got so furious that he started stomping his feet. 'How dare you say we're shirking! And you've served the country? We'll withdraw all our support. Let's see, between you and those volunteer sanghs how many you can make literate!'

These meetings are usually open, informal, and no one bothers with appointing a chair. I generally sit in a corner, and yet I have to mediate quite often. I said, 'You both are making a mistake. This matter is not like someone's daughter's wedding, where the groom's party can leave in a huff, and the bride's father has to deal with the consequences. Step forward only if you think it's a task worth carrying out, a campaign worth mounting. And, please, no one here glares at anyone else. We're not interested in doing a head count, our goal is to build up an informal discussion group in every village and neighbourhood, looking towards the future. For six months now there'll be studying, after that through a solid agenda of post-literacy activities, people will find their own ways to be effective in terms of organized thinking and participation. They'll sit down together here to talk about the various problems of their living and livelihood, to collectively figure out avenues of protest and remedy. From the different positions we hold, we will join this campaign as far as we can; and in this effort please do not let egos come in the way—yours or that of your institution.'

Although our discussion under the bus depot's one and only tarpaulin ended that day with tea and pakoras, there was yet another storm of arguments and discussion on the organization and writing of instructional texts. The village workers called town professors 'urbanites', the left wing student leaders asserted that the panchayat elects were unconcerned with class consciousness. A frightful misunderstanding arose between the art-school principal and the overseer Gyan-babu on the question of the cover picture. And meanwhile Abinash-babu had started collecting, in a thick notebook, songs and poems by folk artists and poets on this subject. Almost every day some new poems reached him by post or by hand, and he would come and read them out to me, either at my office or at home if I got back early enough in the evenings. He was here today, sitting patiently under the jaam tree. I listened to his poems and then saw him off.

At our evening meetings, when I look at all of them in the low-wattage light of the town hall or, with power cuts, in a candle's trembling light and shadow, I see in the changing lines of their faces expressions of anger, anguish, sarcasm, boastfulness, hope and fear. Then it seems to me that, so long after independence, we're preparing together the draft of yet another liberation struggle. What will emerge out of this we don't know—perhaps nothing at all. Maybe all that will remain is a bit of charcoal ash and the murky residue of resolution's near-empty bottle of oil. Almost every day all sorts of problems from distant areas reach us in our control room. In the municipality's ward number three, students have threatened to quit studying unless they get kerosene oil. When I'm asked I'd say, okay, let them quit studying, no one's begging them to study. Immediately, the volunteer worker would change his tone and say, 'No, no, the students didn't say anything, we're the ones with problems.' Then I'd have to tell him the story of Jadumohini's Munda neighbourhood. Together the male-female students and literacy workers buy kerosene from the ten paise per head they save each week out of what they make from selling the kendu leaves they collect. Now who're the poorer, the town-dwelling people of ward three or the folks of Jadumohini?

I don't have to answer this question; Jatin goes back scratching his head. His father and uncle joined up to sell ration-shop kerosene in the black market at every opportunity. Class-consciousness indeed!

All these years nothing has come of pouring in money and offering 'incentives'. If it had, we wouldn't be having to start from scratch. The money got spent. In the official records the statistical accounts have grown like paddy seedlings in monsoon water. Poverty, darkness, high mortality, illiteracy, all the things we've wanted to wipe out. Today, they've all come as volunteers, they're not taking money, rather they're contributing money, so let them ask questions, let them punch holes in our complacent sense of duty. With that, we may not make much progress in statistical terms, but we certainly won't be falling behind as human beings.

Ranadeb Chaudhuri, I hear, has submitted a secret report at the state level. Some of Mahuldiha's social workers are really worried about it. The roadside meetings I hold from time to time, joining knots of people along the way, have apparently provided a quotation or two, which had been embellished and cited in the report.

Apparently the report says that I don't believe in elections, that I'm a communist, and an anarchist. After he finished reading poetry this evening Abinash-babu, looked at me with a worried expression on his face. 'You know, he has written that you're a communist!'

This word has quite another meaning in this area. The urban elite calls someone communist if they want to hit out at them, to throw mud at them. The insinuation is: your name is about to be blacklisted in the police records. Stan D'Souza, for example, must be a communist. The young lecturer who gives free tutorials instead of private tuition after college hours, cannot but be a communist, says the principal Satya Chaudhuri. Why else would he bother to put ideas in the students' heads? In this region, any act of honesty or altruism for which no material end or immediate interest can be found is seen as a symptom of being communist.

Looking at Abinash-babu's worried sunken face, I laughed. 'O Baba, a communist! That's quite a big adjective. But why are you whispering the word like this, as though it had a bad connotation, like a blackmarketeer or broker?'

My reaction worried the old gentleman even more. Seriously he said, 'Please don't talk like that! I want your good, that's why I'm very worried.'

'You needn't worry. It's all right.'

After seeing off Abinash-babu I tried to recall what I might have said about elections. Which statement had Ranadeb Chaudhuri picked out and twisted? Our democracy and election system is something to be proud of—this I've said many times. Oh, yes, I think once I'd said, 'When those who can't even read the names of candidates turn out in large numbers to vote at the bidding of the area's most influential man, then don't you think we ought to work to end this reign of silence?' But that speaks not of lack of belief in the process of election, rather of a profound belief *in* it. From here, sitting at this moment with my eyes closed, I can describe how Ranadeb went red in the face and turning his inflexible huge neck with an effort, said in an emotionally charged voice, 'And yet by saying this sort of thing as the district chief, she insulted hundreds of our supporters, who in spite of their age-old burdens of ignorance, blindness and superstition, have again and again brought about changes at the national and state levels.'

It's quite funny. Ranadeb Chaudhuri at this end, Manmohan Barik at the other, both in despair about my future.

Manmohan, professor of political science, smirking behind his salt-and-pepper moustache, is my teacher's age. So when he looks patronizingly at me over his glasses, asking, 'So, benevolent administrator, how's the reign going?' I can't answer back.

Last time I was in Swarupnagar, I came face-to-face with him at a party. I didn't have the time to argue, I was about to go home, but only if Manmohan would let me off!

'Well Kamalika, now that you and your acolytes have all
the walls covered with your campaign slogans, can you tell me
what can possibly come out of this literacy-schmiteracy? Those
who did the smashing-up in Ayodhya, were they illiterate?
When they are all freed by this so-called mantra of yours, and
all send their children to school, can you accommodate them
in the schools of your district? Will you be able to give all
of them loans, or electricity? Over there, I hear, quite often
there's a continuous power cut; if people ask whether the
vaccines the children are getting have any potency left, how
will you respond? Kamalika, if this is the formula through
which freedom comes, then ha ha to your freedom.'

Quite a few things could've been said in answer to
Manmohan Barik. Just giving him a copy of the poster made
by the art-school students and walking away could've sparked
off fireworks. The red-and-black poster simply says: *Identify
the Enemies of Literacy.*

But the trouble with scholars is that they were born on this
earth to talk, not to listen. And he's not one to concede a point.
So I just smiled and left. Ranadeb or Manmohan, I haven't
gotten round to responding to either one directly. But because
Ranadeb is around, he probably has his answer by now.

On that one night I did see a sort of terror on his face,
in his eyes. There was a relay-procession that would cover
250 kilometres. It would start off from Laxmanpur mouza,
the district's farthest point south-west with twenty-five young
people carrying flaming torches. Sixteen or twenty kilometres
along the way, they'd by joined by youngsters from a nearby
village who would take the torch and start their run, and in
this manner, crossing the highs and lows of the hills, crossing
the Kanika forest, the torch procession would come through
Mahuldiha. Beyond Mahuldiha it would go eighty kilometres

along the highway, then through Lorka, from where it would change direction and head southeast again, to the end of the district in village Rangalata, the last one in Jarangloi subdivision. When the runners passed through human settlements, enthusiastic viewers came out on balconies, in storefronts, the band in the bus-stand's tenthouse struck up, and when they went by a school, the schoolchildren came out holding marigold garlands and strings of paper-cut letters, offering them water and batasa sugardrops. Running along the highway is not that hard. The road underfoot is at least even and clear, though the pitch starts melting under the sharp sun, which they don't mind. But the hardest part is to cover the long stretches of winding and unclear pathways through the nearly impassable hills and forests.

Human habitations are few and far between in these areas. You won't meet with a human face for ten kilometres sometimes. People leave at dawn in search of work, or go to the forest to collect twigs and branches, bamboo shoots, honey, or the saal and the mahua stuff. They return at dusk. And who among them would've had the time to wait by the wayside and welcome these crazy youngsters? It was for this reason that I advised them to end the run at Lorka. Beyond Lorka, the southeast route they had planned to follow is extremely difficult. Especially the patch between the Mahavir and the Kerandimal hills. The forest there is absolutely unbroken, families of leopards play in the open even in the daytime; a she-bear with her cubs may easily appear on the road. Endless stretches of saal, arjun, acacia and teak trees—human eyes become disoriented just looking at that shimmering great screen of yellow and green in mid-day sun. No sound anywhere, only the occasional brush of a leaf falling on the path or a bird calling '*two-ee two-ee*' or a woodpecker's monotonous tapping. Wherever the stream of Champajharan or Jhima happens to dart like a restless girl through the heart of the forest, if you listen you can hear the sound of crystal water in the air! No matter how pleasant this forestland is to look at, it is dangerous for human beings. But the workers who had burnt midnight oil planning this march insisted they wanted to do it. Their argument was that the young people of Mahuldiha weren't going to run all the way, the torch was going to be passed to local people; they knew the paths better, so they were also less afraid. And also, our enchanting river Gurupriya would be on the route!

To reach Jarangloi, the river has to be crossed by boat or motor launch. Listening to the boys talk about it, Bishai got all excited. He's right there of course, sitting in the shed all day. Bishai would swim to midstream and, when the boat was halfway across with the torch, he'd take the torch and swim to the other side, where an army of young people from Jarangloi would be waiting.

He was crazy as crazy can be. The flame must keep burning, it can't be allowed to go out, and how could anyone swim with a flaming torch?

But Bishai wouldn't listen, he'd stand in the water for some time and hold up that torch, or failing that he'd hold it atop his head. How else could it be established that this river was his very own?

So, the boat came close to the other bank, and Bishai standing in waist-deep water took this flaming torch and waded ashore with it. On that day Bishai barely drank, and on his face was the unclouded smile that comes from a full stomach. Of course, if Manmohan Barik hears of this, he'll take a sip of white wine, lean back against the wall and say, 'Rubbish! Symbolism.'

But we aren't bothered by that.

Ranadeb is. The welcoming crowd stood waiting at the crossroads of Mahuldiha. The sky was turning from red to purple, night was about to fall. Over the microphone, in running commentary style someone was giving a description of the route travelled by the relay battalion that was running this way, right from sunrise this morning from Laxmanpur. Unable to overcome either his curiosity or his tension and suspicion, Ranadeb finally got out of his car. He paused for a bit, discomfort clear on his face. For any occasion in this town and bazaar, whether it's the opening of a garage or a public library, the Kumar Bahadur has an invitation. No one had invited him that day. Actually after a while he realized that no one had invited anyone. By then, a noise was audible in the distance, a crowd was moving forward, a rolling wave of posters and banners, and a string of lights flickering in the darkness. The Mahuldiha people who had gone to the city's edge to welcome the procession had a torch each ready in their hands and those were now lit. At once a nameless fear must have run down Kumar Bahadur's spine like an electric shock. For, with a red face and muffled voice, he asked, 'Who're they? What do they want?'

Why does symbolism scare someone so powerful? I wish this question could be put to Manmohan.

Actually, I have often opted out of, the game of questioning and answering. People might say, this doesn't befit you. Power, they'd say, must be asserted every moment, the surest way is to firmly thrust ruthless logic in the face of questions of life and death. I haven't been able to do it. And everywhere I have shown my incompetence in this respect.

When Basumati first came, she asked me with surprise, 'Ma, where's the baby's bottle?'

'She doesn't have her milk from a bottle, Basumati. Take a well-scrubbed steel cup for her.'

She looked doubtful, so I explained the problem with bottles. Germs multiply in milk left at the bottom, at the mouth and nipple. Most of the time I'm away, and a bottle not cleaned carefully enough can give Kuki infections. It's much easier to clean a cup, it doesn't have to be boiled for half an hour like a bottle. How come then bottles and powdered milk reached the village people so easily?

Even though Basumati hadn't asked this question, I could guess it was in her mind. My friend Melanie from England, stayed with me for a few days in Swarupnagar while she was in India. After dinner when I handed her a cup of instant coffee, Melanie broke the protocol of politeness and put it down. 'I'm not going to drink this.'

'Why, what's wrong with it?'

'We've boycotted this company. Don't you know, they're the cause of most infant deaths? How can you, an Indian woman, take it so lightly? Do you know what they do? They send women in white uniforms to the mothers of newborns. Pretending to be nurses, they hand the mothers sample tins of milk powder. The mother starts thinking that breastfeeding is bad for her baby and only powdered milk will help him to become like the baby in the picture on the tin—haven't you heard all this?'

At that time, I hadn't, indeed, thought this matter through. While attending a seminar in Delhi, I had seen a poster of this boycott. There was a picture of a baby kicking a tin of milk powder; and underneath the legend, 'Give Them the Boot'. I didn't think this boycott had anything to do with my habit of drinking a cup of coffee before going to bed.

But after coming to Mahuldiha, I was like someone who

had suddenly woken up, touched by burning fire. I had no idea the problem was so extensive, and had gone so deep.

Kamala, our health worker in Kotasingi took, with heroic effort, two adivasi babies in the last stages of malnutrition to the hospital—though calling this ramshackle place, surrounded by jungle and reached by dirt tracks, a hospital is an over-statement. During the rains, pots and buckets have to be placed on the floor to catch the leaks. And then, the place is twenty kilometres away. Kamala had to plead with a bullock-cart driver to get the two babies to the hospital. But they did not live.

For both, powdered milk had been recommended when signs of serious malnutrition were noticed. That's what the hospital records and the doctor's prescription said. An amazing fact. Before the milk-powder companies were set up, what did babies without access to mother's milk live on? They were fed gruel of broken rice or mandia, dal mixed with rice water, or hand-mashed boiled roots! But these 'old' things are now considered bad for the image of medical science. And so, enter tinned milk. Kamala brought me the documented history preceding the death of two infants. Their village is all of twenty-eight kilometres from the pharmacy in Kotasingi. Two tins had been bought ten or fifteen days earlier by Suka and Bharat Oraon. The label on the tin carried instructions on how much water to mix, and the doctor too explained this to them. In effect, it meant they'd have to come back at the end of one week and spend another forty rupees. Apparently that's why, on the advice of Suka and Bharat, their young wives attempted to stretch the supply from one week to two and a half weeks by cutting down the amount of powder they used. Soon after, the two small lives were on the brink of death from watery diarrhoea. Suka and Bharat had one child each.

Bharat's first baby was a daughter who died at age three, then came this boy. For Suka his son was an only child. Neither can hope for another child. Their wives have been sterilized.

'How could you encourage sterilization in such a case? For a girl of twenty or twenty-two, the mother of one child, that Bhanumati, Suka's wife?'

Embarrassed, the doctor said defensively, 'What can we do? We too need to meet our targets. With the target for family planning the government has assigned us, a case or two of this kind once in a while—'

'Do you know the population growth rate of this community?'

'No, I don't, how can we know each community's growth rate separately?'

'But you do know that in Chaitra-Baisakh their pockets are empty, the paddy all finished, pots and pans mortgaged to pay their debts? And, for the likes of Suka and Bharat at that time, how fatal the temptation of two hundred rupees can be. Getting one's wife sterilized is nothing then, one could be driven to mortgage one's wife—!'

'I'm sorry,' the doctor got up with a sigh, and became busy fiddling with the dispensary's broken refrigerator, and shooing off the mangy dog that lay on the verandah. 'I am under so much pressure all the time,' he said, 'What can I do? The tension is too much. If a patient dies there'll be an attack on the hospital, if a patient is not admitted they'll harass you out there. We have to take flak from both sides.'

Indeed, this machine is so vast, its presence so extensive that if a few hundred lives get squashed under its wheels, who's going to blame whom?

Who will give their lives back to the eighteen year-old unmarried girl or the sixteen year-old boy who have become part of the drive to meet targets, and have lost their right to be parents? Teenage mother Lakhu Mundarin stands waiting, her infant baby in her arms. A medical camp is on under the big banyan tree of Khamarpara. The baby has bad diarrhoea after a bout of measles. It will not even take the breast, it's quite emaciated.

Without adequate medicines, or working equipment, the young doctor Harish Tripathi still sees patients at the camp with a lot of love and care. Examining this baby, Harish gives a start: 'What's this, his eyes are gone!'

The infant boy has gone blind, this happened quite some time ago, Lakhu didn't know. She stares at the doctor with surprise, and says, 'All right, why don't you treat him? Give him medicine.'

'Medicine will not help now. If only you had brought him earlier!'

In a pile there lie the concentrated doses of vitamin A for free distribution. Just twelve spoonfuls fed over five years can prevent blindness from vitamin-A deficiency. The vials are in one place, the people they are meant for are somewhere else. We haven't been able to cross the space separating the two. Lakhu has come again with the baby in her arms, to me in Mahuldiha: 'You help me, the doctor doesn't listen to what I am saying.'

'Lakhu, please go back home. I'm defeated by this. A vagrant beggar can be picked up and held for eternity in preventive custody under rule no. 109, but bringing back lost eyesight, or accounting for this blindness, these I can't do. Instead, you should—!'

'Instead, you should take these with you. What use are these papers to us?' Old Tetri, grim-faced, returned a bunch of green cards tied together with a strip of old sari border to me. The first silent protest from the women of Kureshpur.

After sterilization, sixty percent of them were sick from infections and other complications. No one had provided any follow-up treatment. Forty percent had lost one or more of their children. In the last five years child mortality has not decreased, instead it has gone up by one point. In the statewide competition for sterilization targets, this district has won—and these are the women who were sacrificed in that yagna. Any one who has been sterilized after building a small and happy family of two children is awarded this green card. According to the law, they're supposed to get loans and land if they are landless, and if the son is keen on higher education—

And if the son dies?

Stan has told them in his Kureshpur group meeting. 'Without solving the problem of child mortality, it's not possible to lower the birth rate for poor people. You have to stop becoming targets just because you need money for your immediate needs. To protect your living children should also be the duty of the government!'

With the sharp stare of her clouded eyes old Tetri tried to see into my mind. Then, with her dry stick-like fingers she caressed my cheek and touched my head, saying, 'But our quarrel is not with you. We had to register our complaint, and we did just that.'

Bharat and Suka, Lakhu, old Tetri, I haven't had an answer to give to any one of them, Manmohan-babu. The little I've attempted to do is to let Stan stay with them, bonded in love and trust with them, firmly holding their hands as he has. This is just about what can be taken as my answer.

7

'So, are you happy?' Ajayendra says as he gets up, his fingers sporting astrologer's gemstone rings tap out Morse codes on the desk.

'Why, aren't you happy?'

'Ah, my being happy or unhappy doesn't matter. I'm not a messiah of the poor like you. I've no image to think of. Anyone who has ever had to go to the police station will curse my ancestors fourteen generations up, and anyone who's let off and gets out...!' Ajayendra wags his thumb, 'won't return to say thank you by mistake.'

His amused eyes study the effect of his 'messiah of the poor' on me as he gets up. At the door, he turns back and says, 'Come, let's go out to Chiri. All of us together, to celebrate. Ask Mr. Srivastava. Shyama will also come. We'll take the children along, spending the day out with them, and the night at the guest house, in that beautiful weather in Chin now.'

'What's there to celebrate? Whatever has happened in Chiri, or is going to happen, ought we to take credit for that?'

'No? Who's to take it then? Who got Rupak transferred from there? Had our joint report contested the press report, would the government have taken such prompt action regarding all this improvement? We're the ones who gave it a legitimate appearance, otherwise that agitation of theirs....'

'Ajay, I am really grateful, not because you haven't let the Ignes case go on the charge-sheet, but because you came running here early in the morning to tell me that it hasn't been charge-sheeted. You knew I'd be happy to hear that, right? But, my friend, I've some difficulty taking that credit. Every month a lot of your cases get finally reported, yet in this case, where there really was no serious charge—murder, assault or robbery—against Ignes, you had to be directed from Swarupnagar not to charge-sheet the person.'

Ajayendra's face becomes a shade cloudy. Disappointed, he says, 'I don't like the way you peel and look through everything. If all of us thought like this, we'd never be able to acknowledge any good results in our work. After all, we're just the instruments everywhere. Perhaps things would be less difficult if you didn't take life so seriously.'

After he's gone, I feel a mild prick of conscience. Where was the need to bring up such things? Sometimes it seems I reject peace of mind for myself and don't let anyone else have it either.

I get up and go to the window at the back of the room and look outside. The compound's moss-stained yellow wall comes right up to the window. Beyond the wall is some uneven green ground, and a number of yellow-coloured staff quarters lie scattered far from each other. Beyond these grounds a hint of the forest green edging the city, and further back the Kerandimal hills, stretched out under the sun. A truly lovely day. A bright blue sky, with clumps of autumn cloud hovering close to the hilltop, the colour of sunshine the rich yellow of kolke flowers. Durga-puja is over; it's almost the end of Aswin. The chilly weather waits, crouching like a tiger, it will pounce around mid-Kartik. I've some powerful wrenching memories, connected with this pause between seasons, they often mingle with memories of the city that visits me in my dreams....

Durga Puja just passed; the immersion of the images is over; on the field where the Puja festivities were held the dust is flying and here and there lie scattered saal-leaf plates, eggshells and ice cream wrappers. The colourful fabric of the canopies has been removed, only the skeleton of bamboo and rope stands there, waiting to be pulled down by the decorator's men. The uprooted mast of the merry-go-round has left a huge hole in the centre of the field, like a fresh wound. Underneath the shiuli tree of the school, the ground turns creamy white with the spent blooms it sheds each day. Every year at this time I used to get a fever. The body signalling its rebellion after four-five days of eating nothing but coloured ice, ice cream and fuchka. Just before schools opened, there would be an afternoon when my temperature would rise. In the corner room, with all the windows closed except for a slight gap in one, I'd sit shaking, covered in a sheet, feeling the wind changing direction, sensing the approach of winter. From now on I must come home earlier in the evenings—the sound of the conch blowing in the temple is heard around 5:15 at the head of our lane now. Even as fever grips me, I press my hands close to my nose for the remembered fragrance—once I gathered a lot of shiuli flowers from the school compound, and filled up my folded skirt-front and sprinted all the way home with the orange-yellow from the stems on my fingers....

Today, after a long time, as I stand by the window, I see that soon-to-end autumn day again at the foot of Kerandimal, on this side of its hazy screen of yellow and green.

Today my mind slumps, disabled like a kite with its string broken. Yet, there's no apparent reason, none at all, for feeling sad. Rather, there are a few things worth celebrating.

The telephone call from the boss in the morning.

'Did you know about the drinking water problem in Chiri?'

'Of course!'

'In that case, why didn't you take it up in all this time? I hear that an epidemic can break out anytime in the contract labourers' slum, the water they've been drinking is so bad!'

'I did in fact inform the company four months ago. They did the estimates and said that since the labourers were not their regular employees, it wasn't possible for the company to put in so much investment.'

'You could've reported it to the government!'

'The chief engineer informed me that supplying piped water there was not going to be possible in the next five years, because it is not considered one of the priority areas.'

'Impossible!' I could see my boss sit up in his chair. The chief engineer has informed the government only yesterday—the first phase of the work there will start at the end of this year, because it's a serious problem area.'

'That's good!'

'I thought, since you're so well informed about these difficult areas, you'd be the one to bring up the matter before us! Just saying, "That's good," is not enough! After all, it's a matter of public interest....'

I understood; in this chess game, the representatives of public interest in the capital had made their ultimate move. What I wanted, what Ignes and his group wanted, that's exactly what was being accomplished. So, where's the harm in my accepting this bit of blame, that I hadn't paid enough attention to such a serious matter?

The press report, and the joint report that Ajayendra and I submitted at the legislative assembly, have raised a storm of debate there. In the course of that debate, the question of the contract labourers' miserable living conditions, the pathetic lack of drinking water, medical care, health, schooling, everything came up for discussion. Ignes had sent an open letter to the members of the assembly. That letter clearly stated quite a few problems, and suggested some solutions as well. Of course, all solutions involve money. Who is to spend the money for contract labourers, the company or the government? This was a question that had, in the past, been subjected to a lot of hair-splitting, and the files kept getting heavier with more and more papers but nothing was actually done. Also, this letter from Ignes was printed in the newspapers. Faced with preparing for the upcoming election, the government has suddenly changed its previous, intransigent position. In this quick reversal of events, the minority unions were reprimanded. Why hadn't they taken stock of these aspects of the workers' lives and reported to the government? The ruling party's secretary called an emergency meeting and said, 'All right, let's start with the drinking water. If the company won't pay, we will. Meanwhile, let the company hospital take the responsibility for their medical care. Let a report to this effect be sent to the central government.'

After this resolution was passed unanimously, the chief engineer, left with little choice, reviewed the matter and submitted a new report—especially marking Chiri as a problem area.

Alas, it was right after this session that Ajayendra was directed not to charge-sheet Ignes. Of course, Ajayendra has spared no effort on his part to convince them. As soon as he could sense the approaching change of wind, he slowed down the investigation. And even before that, he took prompt action against the perpetrators of the atrocity. My thanks, Ajayendra. Though our relationship is so informal, yet within that I'll never be able to thank him in words. But, even so, I have not yet reached the state of mind in which I'd like to take off to Chiri for a family picnic.

I've very carefully hidden from the boss the fact that, because I leave my eyes and ears open, I know the history and the interconnectedness of all the decisions the government has taken. He has a sense of self-satisfaction after telling me all that he wanted to. Just this little window of self-satisfaction is very important for him, standing as he does, in constant tension, in the space between me and the government. That I understand. Still, my mind continues to feel somewhat disabled.

Rajat was away in Delhi for a meeting between a World Bank group and his department, concerning a project of theirs. Even though this area is not under his jurisdiction, still Rajat knows I'd be happy to hear of it so he came at noon and gave me the good news. The forest ministry, apparently, has finally approved the forest department's proposal. Their letter is on its way. This means that work on the bridge on that enchanting river of ours bordering Jarangloi will now be rapidly finished. The framework of the bridge is complete but the approach road was held up. Because the road has to cut through a forest area—though only on paper, what the eyes see is just an empty stretch of stony arid highland—the forest ministry could not approve it without getting some forest land in exchange for this land. The accounts on this have finally been closed. The road construction itself won't take very long. It only remains for the tender to be offered. Once the bridge is complete, the two banks will be linked. People won't have to risk their lives crossing back and forth. For this harvest season, of course, the towed platoon of boats will operate, but by the end of winter the fair-weather road will be set. And next year, about this time, the bridge will be all ready. The people and the authorities in Lorka and Mahuldiha will no longer be able to neglect the other side of the river as if it were an untouchable....

One person will suffer a lot, of course. Bishai Munda. He'll have to leave the riverside shed and find some more, complicated way to survive. This bridge will completely change the very meaning of survival for him. The launch will be discontinued; the shed become home for stray dogs and beggars. Bishai's everyday games with the river: standing in the neck-high wild black water; the pull that drew him out of his home day after day to sit at the boat landing; the way night after night, not caring for female company, he has wrapped the strong river wind around his bare body, wet and muddy from head to toe—will the musk of that attraction let go of him? Perhaps Bishai will have to move elsewhere in some brick kiln as a labourer, or become bonded in labour to a creditor in the next village, but his heart's longing will stay afloat on the river's black water like a shaft of moonlight!

I too will be left missing something, the memory of crossing the roiling water with its sinuous flow. To watch the river from the bridge, that too is a kind of relationship. But it does not have this overwhelming attraction. I'm standing on the bridge alone at night; the moonlight around me like a flowering paddy field; visible farther down the river is the sandbar, pale, bare, secluded; on the banks a sleeping village here, the flapping of a nightbird's wings in a forest there; the water flowing with a soft, almost muffled, sound and the thin reflection of the moon as it splinters on the water. I can see the scene right now in my mind's eye. And with that I feel a keen desire for physical union with the river, water. But all this is just romance which doesn't do much for practical things. I've promised the people of Jarangloi that I'll do all I can to make sure the bridge is completed as soon as possible. So, for the time being, I'll just set aside this angst like a folded up shawl.

Twice Basumati has paused at the door of my office, hesitantly giving me a signal. The office is adjacent to the residence, the jaam tree before the house visible from the office window. It's two-thirty in the afternoon, long past lunchtime. That's what Basumati is trying to bring to my attention.

What sort of childishness am I indulging in? Who am I upset with that I'm doing without food? I keep thinking that the telephone hasn't rung. Today is my birthday. At least a telephone call was due from Swarupnagar. Perhaps Guddu could have talked for a while, and then Ranjan, no matter how remote he stays. If for just a few seconds on this one day his voice was to shed a few drops of dew, what harm could it do anyone? I feel particularly chastened because, becoming impatient, I called Swarupnagar a couple of hours ago. But there was no answer. They're not home. It's a regular working day, not a holiday. So Guddu is at school and Ranjan is in the office. It was a mistake to call them at home—so I dialled Ranjan's office number. He wasn't there either. Suddenly I've thought of Somnath. Maybe Somnath has turned up like a shadow figure, at the school or in Ranjan's office. And that has led to some sort of danger or tension.... I feel a little apprehensive....

I'm so far from home; Ranjan knows this is one day on which I don't like to float like this, roots severed. When I was little, there was no tradition of celebrating birthdays in our home. At school sometimes we'd see people wishing each other or sending cards. Ranjan is the one who taught me, in his own way, how to discover the joys of a birthday amidst the pressure and tension of our lifestyle. No cake-cutting, no party, just lighting oil lamps at home, planting a tree or two, having a picture taken, alone and with the others, taking a walk in the evening somewhere quiet. Just this. So much loveliness mixed with this unceremonious celebration, revisiting old memories during the walk. My childhood in Calcutta, Ranjan's adolescence in Patna, his childhood in Muzaffarpur. After that, skipping the few years of my messed-up shame-filled life in Delhi, then suddenly meeting Ranjan in a train....

I have done the strangest thing, just to prove my stubbornness. It was exactly on this day last year that I left Swarupnagar early in the morning to come here. Swapno had just wiped the sleep from his eyes and picked up his glass of milk. Kuki was still sleeping. A ten-hour journey ahead. I was going for the first time. If I started any later it would mean I'd reach there at night—this was the rationale I had given to Ranjan. Ranjan said he had to attend an urgent meeting that day; if I waited till the next day, he would come with me. I didn't pay any heed to his suggestion. That morning, when he woke up Ranjan didn't say anything to me, but the hint of a cold smile stayed on his lips. At that time I thought it was a smile of sarcasm. Today it seems he had to wear that smile all the time in order to deceive the people around us. A complex push-pull process of various emotions was going through my mind. The tension of going so far from home, the anxiety about adapting to a new situation, and above all, the terrible pain of going away from Swapno. Couldn't Ranjan have asked me even once more to stay on that day and start the day after? When the car left Swarupnagar and took the national highway, my vision suddenly blurred with tears.

Just one year. The earth has been able to circle the sun just once. The planets farther away in the solar system will take even longer to complete this cycle. After autumn mornings laden with the fragrance of siuli flowers, has come the hemanta season—of brilliant blue skies, the vibrant yellow of flowering mustard fields, and the thinning river. And then, with the wind's changing direction, the palash, shimul and krishnachura trees on both sides of the road have broken into a riot of efflorescence. The lone kusum tree, comely in red foliage, has stood in the middle of the field like a princess on swayamvara. The summer has come, the harsh sun, the cracking of earth underfoot. Blazing hot winds race through the forest, leaving a wake of fires in their trail, the hills awake all night, wearing that eerie garland of small fires. Then the rain. The smell of baked earth getting its first soaking; the rain's waving fringe seen crossing the Kerandimal hills and running this way; the river swollen from streams of water running in from all sides; I standing in the rain in the dark, looking for a light on the bank. And then, finally, a sky spent with giving rain, the earth at the end of the cycle. Again the autumn has come, bringing with it a touch of chill....

The nature that surrounds me—these forests, hills, the river, I find they all seem to have this lively rhythm in just being there. How easily their faces change in different lights, how effortlessly they take off and put on the adornments of different seasons! Though I live right in their midst, my movements have not acquired any ease or rhythm. That fourteen year-old Babli's awkward stumbling walk wearing a sari has not changed. Why must so many rocks be scattered in my path everywhere? As though I were a soldier in a frontier war. Sometimes at the sight of an empty field, I try to run all the way to the horizon—worn out again from battle, the next day I retreat a mile and a half. Sometimes the fight with the antagonist goes on all night for just the tiniest bit of earth—as much as a needle can hold on its head, and then waking in the morning I find only sunshine on my forehead, the opponent having departed, leaving me to sleep. Each day I get defeated, and set out again on march. Each day I move forward, then retreat again. In precisely this manner, the history of this war is mapped out in my own bloody footprints.

Like that time, last Saturday, when I was returning from Tirki. By the time I left it was quite late. Tirki's modal and his associates just wouldn't let me leave....

There was an old out-of-order lift irrigation point which had been lying unused for a long time in the jungle around the Lunavasa ditch. It had been perhaps thirty years ago. The village elders say that over one 150 acres of land used to be cultivated with its help for the rabi crops, so strong was the spring's supply of water. The motor had developed some minor problem. At that time the water cooperatives had still not come to this area, and so there was no liability procedure. Afraid to bear the brunt of the blame, the villagers avoided running the point any more. Applications were submitted repeatedly to the relevant department in Mahuldiha. This year, money was sanctioned for installing a new point but, based on the argument that there was no money for repairing old points, those applications were being put to sleep inside files. Slowly the pipes got stolen, a piece or two at a time. No one paid that project any serious attention. The strange economics of our accounting remains quite beyond me. Which is greater: the value of the crops that could've been raised on this land in the past twenty rabi seasons or the one and a half lakh rupees in repair costs? When I asked this, I was told that calculating the value of the crop was the agricultural department's job; we're the irrigation department, why should we do the comparisons? However, the headman of Tirki did just that, which later on became a most potent weapon. Along the road to Lorka, about twenty kilometres short of it, there's a finger of an old road going towards Tirki. There, at the crossroads, blocking my passage, the modal was waiting with a large number of people as well as drums, bullhorns etc. Making a great deal of noise, and stirring up a lot of dust, the crowd almost hijacked me and took me to the out-of-order lift point. After that began a winning phase in our history of battles.

The seniormost irrigation officer for this district had already rejected Tirki's demand a long time ago. When the counterattack came again from me, he said in distress, 'Please, make no such commitment, there isn't enough money, it can't be done even in the next year, certainly not this year.' At that point, Amulya the young overseer spoke to his boss diffidently, 'If you allow me, I can give it a try. Actually it's not as expensive as it seems. We need to check a bit on the details.'

For the last two and a half months, this young man has laboured with his heart and mind in this obscure part of Tirki, amidst jungle and water. Working through rain

and shine, he has redone the map of the pipeline. Most
of the route was thickly covered in wild vines and shrubs,
the modal's men stayed with him clearing overgrowth and
preparing a path. Amulya carefully checked each piece of
machinery that lay in disuse at the site, he searched their
own workshop storage for spare parts. Finally one day,
cutting through the red tape, the solution landed in our
laps like a perfectly round apple. Amulya did it. This very
young man without a lot of experience accomplished what
no one had done in the last thirty years. Indeed, he did what
no one thought was possible. A small event. A little trick of
project planning. Last Saturday we had to go back there, at
the invitation of the men and women of a village never ever
mentioned in the papers. In the afternoon's strong light, the
oldest farmer Johon pressed the switch to turn on the motor.
In all this land lying unused and barren for some twenty
years, Johon too has a small share. The moment the flow
of water leapt out like a white horse from the pipehead,
the dancers glided into action: arms around each others'
waists they danced through the entire village like two long
colourful garlands, and between them another wild bunch
played their instruments.

From time to time, without altering the rhythm even
slightly, the dancing young girls pulled in the slightly older
wives, young mothers with babies at the breast, who smiled
shyly as they joined the group. Some with a sleeping baby
tied on the back, the baby swaying in its sleep as the mother
danced, a small vine on a tree, dreaming perhaps of a
wondrous swing. Clay pots of mahul liquor were kept under
the trees; every now and again someone would split off from
the group, and take a few quick gulps before joining again.
When Tirki's modal, Jewel, a skinny old man, his rope-like

body seasoned in much sun and rain, came out of the group and took my hand, I had no idea that his drunken body had the strength of ten buffaloes. My awkward steps, the group's rapid rightward thrusts, had them all laughing uncontrollably. The entire chain would move to the right with the song's rhythm, pause a bit, move again— with the group facing it moving left in a similar manner. The pull of the movement was quite something; yes, it felt like being submerged upto the waist in a river as the tide rises, being carried off by a sudden sharp current. High in the sky was a close-to-full tenth-night moon, and under the star-studded sky they danced. Amulya too was dancing, his clothes splattered with mud, his hair dishevelled, his movements rather tipsy. It wasn't easy getting out of this kind of grand assembly; the chief wouldn't let me leave without eating. Not to hurt his feelings, I had to use Kuki as an excuse, my baby girl alone at home, and only then was I allowed to go. I got back on the road, towards Lorka. The rows of trees alongside cast shadows upon the road, and looking ahead at that long, moving carpet patterned in light and shadow my eyes were in a trance. Surely, the line-up of lovely trees was waiting for the dance to start!

On the by-pass, just as we were leaving Lorka behind, I suddenly thought of something, and Adil's face appeared in my consciousness. It was nearly two and a half months since his death. I hadn't been to Lorka in this time. Going there at this time in the ghostly silence of closed mines would, of course, be a kind of lunacy, especially when Kuki was waiting at home. But something was pulling me, hard, an invisible indescribable something.

As we reached the mining zone and Sanatan slowed the car a bit, he turned back and said, 'Ma, can you hear it?' I suddenly had goosebumps all over my body.

This late in the night, work was still going on in the mine. The road was slightly elevated here, and looking in the distance I could see the dumper slowly advancing, the dredger running, the mechanical shovels like giant animals picking up chunks of rock and loading them in the dumper; human figures were also moving about like shadows, carrying pickaxes and crowbars—everything moving, yet silent, no human noise reached the ears, nothing except the faint sound of running machinery. The incongruent mixing of moonlight and the nighttime floodlights gave the scene a sort of other-worldly, ghostly appearance.

I was really stumped. Even under normal conditions, I had never heard of the Lorka mine running night shifts, the management had never agreed to it even when the workers demanded it. Two day-time shifts were all. So what was this? Why were these people working at night?

I came home full of doubt and apprehension. The next day was a Sunday. Normally I try not to disrupt others' lives on this day. I have to work, but that's my fault. This Sunday, however, I couldn't help myself. I sent for Rao, the assistant labour commissioner. Rao was a bit embarrassed that I had found this out before he had been able to hand in a written report.

After Adil's and his wife's agonising deaths from near-starvation and anxiety, and the departure of many other workers from Lorka, the rest managed to survive a couple more months doing assorted farm labour in the rice-planting season of Asarh-Sravan. Those from other districts or provinces sent their wives and children back to their home villages—sent them back to die as well, perhaps after more prolonged partial starvation. Finally, a patchwork solution came down from the management. A new company in

Madhya Pradesh would buy limestone from Lorka; but because it's new, the accounts would be delayed; the Lorka workers would get paid not weekly but monthly; the supervisors would keep weekly records; and there'd be just one shift a day. The crippled union didn't agree to this. The workers, because of this uncertain payment situation, did not want to lose part of their daytime work-hours. Each one had hungry mouths to feed at home, so they'd do day-labour work in surrounding villages—collecting wood, kendu leaves, saal seeds from the forest, while the women collected cowdung for fuel chips—and then, after they'd spent the day scrounging for a living, they'd work at night, so that it wouldn't hurt them as much if their wages were overdue.

I understood the extreme helplessness of a cornered position under which the union had agreed to this arrangement.

'You agreed to this as well, and you didn't brief me earlier?' At that moment I hated Rao with all my heart.

'Please, there was nothing else we could do; I've explored the prospects with the steel company, even the village development schemes in your jurisdiction—but we're talking about four or five hundred workers, their problems are not temporary, they can't leave the colony and move elsewhere, they're caught in the orbit of this mine; even if they go away for the day, they come back at night. Even if they could be settled elsewhere…it's only after thinking all this, Kamalika-devi, that I agreed. On Friday they started working, I just couldn't come earlier and let you know. Before I could come…'

Rao's face reflected a kind of desperate helplessness. I felt a little awkward and said, 'No, no, what difference does it make if I found out? What's done is done!'

Grasping the edge of the table with both his hands Rao said, 'But I give you my word, they'll get their payment by the end of the month somehow! We can start right away setting up contact with Madhya Pradesh, everything is still not lost, Madam.'

I didn't tell Rao that something invaluable was, in fact, lost. Once, when I was going from Khamarpara to Lorka well past midnight, I had talked for hours with these people. They weren't letting go of the bodies of Adil and his wife, not by any means. Not their union. 'Let the bodies decompose, let an epidemic break out in Lorka, we're going to die anyway.' In the light of a gas lantern, amidst the smoke from bidis, I watched their senior leader Asif's frown grow deeper.

What was I doing there? I wasn't from any of the parties involved. The management executives had left to save their skins. The managers like Kureshi, Ojha, who stayed on— they were trembling with fear. Rao, pale in the face, was repeatedly saying, 'Madam, take along a protection force if you must go there, they're really worked up, things can take a wrong turn in this situation and anything can happen—'

Adil, his smile, his light-hearted, easy attitude to life, the memory of his joyous face had, like an undertow, taken me to Lorka that night. I had gone alone, empty-handed.

I gave them a detailed account of what we had done so far to save the mines, and what else could be done in future. Finally, when all this proved fruitless, I brought up the question of rest for Adil's soul; how bad Adil's relatives and friends would feel later if the last rites remained undone and his body decomposed. Partly from the exhaustion of staying up all night, partly from the labour of arguing and reasoning, Asif finally agreed to release the body as the light of dawn started to fill the sky. Some family members and other villagers came from Tenalong, Adil's village, twenty-two kilometres north of Lorka. Adil's wife's parents were both dead. His old father couldn't come. Hiring a tempo, they took the bodies so that they could perform the last rites themselves. Even when faced with a blind alley, Asif had stood his ground that night, guarding the organization's values. In sorrow, in suffering, they had held together. Asif has become very alone in the bare-handed fights against their economic blockades. No sudden turn of wind has changed the situation; nor does our country have any social security for workers in such situations. And yet, these several hundred families have refused to move elsewhere even for a short while. Spending all day in search of work, they've come back home at dusk to this dark colony—in the hope that something will improve, that the situation will change in some way.

The night's darkness has, in a sense, also been able to cover the shame of their defeat today—is that why the union agreed to work at night? Actually, the shame does not belong to Asif and his people, it is ours.

Back in the office after the delayed lunch, I haven't paid attention to anything and dusk is now giving way to night.

Animesh has stayed on all the while. Towards the end of the day, I notice Jatin-babu hovering by the door and call him in. 'What's the matter?'

'I bought some vegetables and stuff from the Tuesday market. If you could let me take off a little early.' I can see that the bag on his side is quite full. Some wooden toys peeping out of the top, perhaps for his grandchildren, a packet of incense sticks—my noticing these seems to increase Jatin's embarrassment.

'That's fine, you can go.'

Everyone has a face behind the mask. After they get out of their office clothes, these individuals working close to me can go back to their natural lives, as someone's father, someone's grandfather, or someone's brother. The inordinate happiness Jatin derives from working in a lungi with his chest bare, trowel in hand, squatting in his sliver of a garden, bears no comparison with what he feels in following me even to win a kingdom, for this happiness he does not earn on his own.

But it doesn't seem I'll ever be able to take off this battle armour and helmet. These have melded with my body, their metallic presence mixed in my blood. Just as my face has gradually become the mask, or the mask the face. Even at home I can no longer spend a self-contained life of ease as Guddu's and Kuki's mother and Ranjan's wife. In the middle of the night, in the midst of reading fairy tales, or disrupting love's embrace, the telephone can ring, and that can mean Ajayendra, or Rajat, or Kumardihi's deputy general manager, or....

Jatin, lowering his face, looking almost at the floor, says, 'Ma, aren't you going home?'

'No, no, I'll be a little late.'

Somewhat desperately he says, 'Why don't you go, Ma, you too go home.'

Jatin isn't given to breaking the bounds of propriety this way. Animesh too has stepped inside, a shy smile on his face. Suspecting something, I get up. Opening the door I look towards the verandah of the house. At once, the whole day's melancholy is gone and a strange sense of wellbeing spreads through my body. Today's my birthday.

Ranjan has come, I can see him, his back—in his deep blue shirt—turned towards the office, his hands in the pockets of his trousers. Swapno and Kuki are playing on the verandah.

Swapno carries Kuki on his back for some distance, then drops her on to the rope cot that is kept on one side.

They suddenly notice me. In surprise they freeze like a still shot in a film.

Then, laughing, they start running this way.

8

'Are you crying?' He asks me, his voice mild, calm.

In response I place my right hand on his cheek, the fingers of my left hand wet from my tears. It is late in the night. The ancient fan hangs from the very high ceiling. There is no sound in the room except the rasp of its turning blades. Swapno and Kuki are asleep in the next room, Basumati on the floor there, on the rolled-out mat.

On other nights the blue light is on, tonight the room is absolutely dark.

With his warm fingers Ranjan touches my brows, the wet eyelids, cheeks, chin and, finally, the lips, one at a time, my body taking in his touch after a long, long time. An endless stretch of time, as though a plateau of lifeless time lay between us. Curving along its edges we went on, each with respective life, never daring to attempt to cross the barrier.

I kiss each one of Ranjan's reclusive fingers separately, solely. Then with friendly ease I call his hand, take it where a decade ago he gave me his first kiss. Unfailing aim.

The wall of obscured glass that had stood behind me, stupidly and needlessly causing confusion, shatters into pieces, producing a liquid music.

'Ranjan, why didn't you tell me earlier? For two years we suffered so much for no reason. The unnecessary misunderstandings, so much time wasted, so many days of our life!'

'Yes, we have certainly suffered,' Ranjan now turns on his back, looking up at the ceiling, both hands under his head. 'But, Babli, the time hasn't been wasted. Once in a while, we also need to search within and find ourselves. After a storm there's so much debris of dust and twigs left around. And, can everything be talked about at any and every time? Each admission that's to be made has its own time, its own moment.' Pausing, he turns to me with a quiet smile.

'Basically the way it goes, you know, is that though I may not be as sensitive as you are, or as emotional, I've tried to follow one rule, especially in moments of crisis. Babli, give the other side scope for self-defense before making up your mind that it's guilty. That helps straighten out a lot of twisted things eventually. Most of the time people presume: being insulted, being tormented. The sorrow of it makes them completely blind. They can't even see the faces of those who're close to them, who have silently endured the same pain. You did know, didn't you, that my point of pride was that I'd never seek bail in your court; and if that means judicial custody, so be it!'

I am back on that night two years ago, carefully turning and examining each ruined moment, in case some life has somehow lingered in the wreckage! Uttara, Uttara Deshmukh. I'll never meet this girl now. If my resentment, sorrow and despair subjected her soul to invisible flogging in the last moments before it left her body, I beg her forgiveness. After all this time. That memory of the time at Kuki's birth still burns me, brings tears that keep soaking my left hand and the sari over my chest.

'What could make a better present on your birthday, tell me? So this time I came on my own, empty-handed.' Ranjan, of course, hasn't come empty-handed, the smell of the flowers he brought flows like a river in darkness. Roses, rajnigandhas. I love flowers more than anything else. *Won't you look at me and see if you can recognize me!* Reciting just this one line of the song he translated in English, he said, 'I don't remember the rest. In poetry I'm not that....'

This was how Ranjan started talking, with humour.

Throughout, he didn't let his mild, disciplined and unemotional way of talking change one bit. So that the tone of his voice didn't hint at any of the inner torment he has had to deal with.

'At that age I didn't have either the intelligence or the empathy to realize that Uttara loved me. I had left Patna and gone to Delhi, I had started my life there with a new job. Uttara had finished her studies in architecture and gone back to Nasik. I do not know if she made any attempt to find me. Young love perhaps disappears like mist with sunrise. At least, it disappears from the eyes. Maybe it takes some form unknown to the senses. Besides, I had found you then. Constantly thinking of how I could heal your cuts and tears, those wounds from the past.... After a long, long time I got a letter. From Uttara's mother. Perhaps Uttara had told her about me. Her mother got our Swarupnagar address from a friend in Delhi—probably even without Uttara's knowledge. The letter had their phone number on it. Uttara hadn't married. In a village near Nasik, a local volunteer organization was raising an orphan adivasi boy. With information from an adoption agency, Uttara adopted that boy. That was quite a few years ago. That two year-old boy, Sirish, is now just over seven. Two and a half years ago, Uttara was diagnosed with stomach cancer. She had gone to Bombay for treatment when a specialist there handed her the death sentence, giving her six more months to live. The cancer was quite advanced. There was not much that could be done. She took a transfer to their company's Swarupnagar branch. It's a small branch, someone of her senior position rarely comes there. That was right after her diagnosis. What a foolish, stubborn girl, you see, Babli. She had my address, but she didn't contact me. I don't know what she had in mind, terribly hurt as she was. That I'd be startled to read of her death in the local papers one day—is that what she wanted? Whatever, it wasn't possible for her mother to stay silent. She used some excuse to go to Delhi to see her son. With a lot of effort she managed to get hold of my address and quickly wrote me a letter. It had one request, that I'd give Uttara the impression that I had found her. I must not mention her mother, Uttara would then never forgive her.

When I'd last seen Uttara, she was a second-year student of architecture. Pale eyes, pale hair, two straight plaits, not very tall, a complexion.... I can't figure out how, so much obstinacy and false pride could be packed like gunpowder in that small person.... anyway, I went to their place. My acting was more or less faultless, Uttara did not sense her mother's plot. After that, I went there a few more times. Her condition was rapidly getting worse. Dark patches under the eyes were getting deeper, she lost a lot of hair from the chemotherapy. She was emaciated and in so much pain that often she couldn't sleep all night. Once or twice, if she felt better, during the day she tried going to the office. But she couldn't keep that up, even that small bit of strain was too much and within an hour the office car would bring her back. That's the time when I wrote down her phone number on the first page of the directory—you remember that?

Yet, I couldn't tell you anything about it, Babli. Dr Basu said your blood pressure was already on the high side from the pressures at work and other tensions, that it was important to keep you cheerful, not to let you get upset or depressed. You might remember, at that time I would often turn the TV off if it showed excessive violence or anything like that.

That was a terrible time for me. On the one hand, a tiny life was growing within you, taking shape bit by bit—though I had never thought of Swapno as someone else's, still Kuki was mine, our first child. On the other hand, Uttara was withering away right before my eyes. I didn't want to worry you, so I would come home after briefly visiting Uttara after office. Then again, lying down beside you while you slept I tossed about, sleepless all night, thinking of Uttara. I couldn't control myself. Saying I needed to go to office early, I'd skip dropping Swapno to school and go to their house. What can it be called, Babli? Sin? Love? Hiding the truth?

Those who lose their temper easily, cry easily, laugh easily, they're lucky, they're happy. I know that now. At least by sharing their inner tension with others, they can somehow unburden themselves. By nature I'm terribly reticent; just as I haven't been able to laugh and table-thump, so even in sorrow I haven't known the good fortune of leaning my head on someone's shoulder. Don't be angry, not even on your shoulder! It has never occurred to anyone to ask what I do when I bleed within. Where would I run?

Most of the time Uttara lay in bed, I sat nearby in a chair, holding her hand. Just that. Perhaps I was trying to see if some powerful mantra could transfer her suffering to me, so she could find a little relief. As you know well, I don't have any talents. I can't sing, I can't write poetry, I can't even recite poetry. It never quite occurred to me that in life there could be a major need for these. I studied, played tennis, did my training, then I took up a job—that's all. But with Uttara I realized how useful those talents would have been. Physical pain you can't wipe away easily, but a song, a poem, a beautiful sentence can sometimes act like a little pebble and push the pain outward into wider circles, at least for a little while.

I remembered something I had learned a long time ago. I was then going to school in Patna. My uncle's guru once came and stayed at our house for some time. He taught me and my elder brother a technique of breathing in and out deeply and quietly. How to concentrate all of the mind solely on the process of breathing in and out. In this way, supposedly, it's possible to get the mind beyond physical pain and conquer bodily suffering. I tried to teach Uttara the little I knew of this method. Perhaps it's all psychological, still it felt good when her mother called me at office the next day and said she had slept four or five hours the night before, peacefully, after a long time. Her mother too must have become exhausted from staying up night after night.

There was no one else. Everything depended on her. There was a maid, but it was Uttara's mother who fed and bathed her, and stayed close to her the whole time. Uttara wanted to die at home, she said she felt suffocated at the hospital.

Think of the curious turn of events; perhaps it's from the pressure of these factors that in her last moments she couldn't find my office number. And, she had been told not to call at home. But she was forced to do so because her daughter's illness was then in its last stages, but she unwittingly gave you such a misleading message that...'

'Let's not talk about it, Ranjan.'

'Why not? Think about it, all our misunderstanding, my

subsequent reaction, everything started from that point. Well! And then, you know what followed!'

'No, what happened to Sirish? And when did Uttara…'

'The night you went to hospital alone, so very upset with me, and kept thinking of the social embarrassment even before seeing the newborn's face, that very night I had to decide the sequence of where to go—first to Uttara's house, then to the cremation ground, then at the very end, after a bath and change of clothes, to the hospital!'

'Going to Kuki's cradle, I thought: what was lost was over, at least there'd be time now to think about living all over again. But that's not how it went. You hurled such a deadly barb of distrust and suspicion at me that everything fell apart. I felt angry with you, felt terribly wronged. I withdrew myself completely and retreated into a small corner of our life.'

'You didn't tell me what happened to Sirish.'

'O yes, Sirish. Uttara's other big regret. Till the end she couldn't get over the fact that Sirish had to be left behind in the same orphanage. Her elder brother in Delhi did not want to take responsibility for the boy. Had it been his sister's own child, he'd have felt an obligation. But this one started an orphan, at most he'd be an orphan again. Uttara's mother could not oppose her son. After her daughter's death, his home was her only shelter. Perhaps that was a major reason…. But, without even informing you, yet knowing very well that you'd never refuse, I gave my word to Uttara that we, I mean you and I, we'd bring him over here. He'd grow up with Swapno and Kuki. This much we had to do, don't you think? Yesterday, I called Nasik and talked with them. Of course, the formal paperwork for adoption etc., will have to be prepared first, whatever little time that takes…. You're crying?'

The mild, calm voice. In answer, I place my right hand on his cheek. The fingers of my left hand are wet with tears.

After so long I'm feeling sleepy, my eyelids are closing, sleep envelopes my whole being. Why am I this sleepy? Have I not slept all this time? Sinking into Ranjan's embrace, I sleepily say to him, 'Tomorrow I'll take you all to see the river.'

In the morning, it's hardly nine when Ajayendra turns up with Shyama. She looks gorgeous. Her husband's success, the prestige of his position, all this seems to be radiating from her person. The beloved of her husband. In a zari-bordered south-Indian silk, liberally sprayed with perfume, she wears a set of gold bangles in a new design round her wrists. Waving her smooth, rounded arms, glancing charmingly sideways, Shyama demands like a girl coming of age.

'I won't take no for an answer. You too must come to Chiri, with us. We're going in our car. Come, we'll have a picnic.'

'Ah, Shyama,' Ajayendra mildly scolds his wife, having perhaps instructed her not to mention Chiri to me.

Polite exchanges with Ranjan, tea drinking, the children being noisy—when all this has subsided, Ajayendra gets up and says, 'Must push off. Or we'll be late getting there. The children are with us.' Then, thinking of something, standing right there at the threshold, he throws a bomb in my direction. With slightly raised eyebrows, he says to Ranjan, 'Do you know, Didi never trusts me? For the last six months we've been watching a certain young man. When I told her that, she almost stopped talking to me. This time, will you praise my good sense, or won't you?'

Apprehensively I said, 'What happened, Ajay? Anything against Stan...'

'I don't know the details. I've to stop by Kumardihi on the way. I told the officer not to arrest the young man until

I'm back. Just sit him down and ask some questions, none
of the third-degree stuff! I told him that on top of being an
engineer, he's your acquaintance. But I'll say this: looking at
the outside, the shell, offers no clue to the reality inside. This
is why I never approved of all this open free mixing in their
organization. Arre baba, these things are possible in U.K.
or U.S.A. Young men and women staying at the same place,
being trained together. This is a rural area. Talk about fire
and ghee, protector and predator—'

'What happened, Ajay?'

'Last evening, Stan brought a girl to his room and raped
her. The girl belongs to their own organization. Jhumur Tirki.
I hear, she's quite smart and clever, studied upto class eight.
But who knows how this—'

'Has the girl made a statement?'

'No, her father has. The girl is not in the village. Her family
probably moved her somewhere to avoid people talking.'

Forgetting all thoughts of the push-pull of mask-helmet-
armour, completely ignoring the fact that Ranjan, Kuki,
Guddu and the two other children and Shyama are staring at
me, I start crying like a school girl. And grasping Ajayendra's
hands, I plead desperately, 'Ajay, please give me your word,
that without talking to the girl, you won't let any case be filed.'

Ranjan is stunned. Ajayendra is in distress. Poor man, he
had no idea my reaction would be like this. Taking a step
back, he pulls out a handkerchief from his pocket, offers it to
me and says in a mildly scolding tone, 'What's this? Dry your
eyes! Is this my father's estate that I can dispense favours?
How can there be a case without a statement from the girl
herself? She's of age. However, the local M.L.A., the Block
chairman and Ranadeb, the three of them have started putting
pressure on us. Saying, the young man is turning the adivasis'

heads, throw him out of here soon. If he can be arrested, it will undermine the trust he enjoys and he'll be forced to move out of here. This is their strategy. The phone call from headquarters came this morning, asking me to investigate the case myself and after filing the case and arresting him, to report back by this evening. You see, Madam?'

'But then,' Ajayendra smiles with a wink, 'I'm not in the least bit bothered by that.' With perfect style he takes out his packet of imported cigarettes, and balancing one between his left index and middle fingers, with his right hand he takes his handkerchief from me and carefully folds it back. 'Whatever I do, I'll do it looking at these tears, and strictly along the line of law. I promise.'

Ajayendra's blue Maruti van rolls out of our gate and disappears in the crowd on the road.

To this day, I haven't been able to forget that river. Over my head now the cruel yellow sunshine, the noise around and the billowy crowd pull me along. Waiting to cross the road on Esplanade east, I look around and notice: this city is laughing, while scattering people everywhere, expelling them like teased-out cotton from balls, exploding. I cross the street without any effort, like a straw atop a wave, with the others, a collectivity of strangers. Ahead of me, in the cobweb of dusty, disused wires of aging trams is trapped part of the western sky, where each day of this spring I see the play of colours just before the sun sets. At this point, my eyes somehow get hooked onto some pattern of clouds in the distance. As though they weren't clouds, but a distant land with a certain sleepy range of hills, where dawn arrives with the smell of mahul! At once, that enchantress appears before me, overflowing the banks of a discoloured sky; her sun-splashed water before my entranced eyes, the yellow-ochre sandbar. As though all the time she were here, right before my eyes, hidden by a sleight of hand in the shuffling of day and night scenes. Then I come to realize that this river, this sun-scented beauty, has me bound in her million spells. I've actually left her realm long ago—but she won't let me go, easily! The four doors of her magic arena closing around me, she'll drown me at day's end in the maze of her blury mirror.

So many times at midnight, or even later, her hypnotic call has followed me in moonlight. Etched against the sky is the city's silhouette, the halogen lights strong enough to dull the stars. A baby crow in the neem overhead caws in its sleep. Then, all of a sudden, like a tune drifting from afar, she comes and lodges in my bloodstream and refuses to let go. At once, wiping off the geometry of the city's night-body, appears the blue-gray firmament stretching to the horizon. Instantly, eager stars in their thousands begin to shine in the mind's eye and, shivering at the unreal call of nightbirds atop the forest, I look up. There she is, spanning the horizon, the bandit woman—the sound of her laughter rings out in darkness!

She's here, this river has been with me, never letting me out of her sight; that's why today it amuses her to suddenly tear through the backdrop of crowd and concrete and flash before my eyes.

Bending over my writing and frowning, Kuki remarks, 'Oh Ma, you wrote exactly the same thing at the beginning. And now you're writing it again? That's repetition!'

Precocious girl, the opinions of the fourteen year-old Kuki or Rhitali can no longer be ignored. In the last two years she's

shot up in height, and is almost as tall as me now. A headful of
wild hair, and glasses on her eyes, since last year. So thin, it's
hard to believe that when she was a baby, each time I picked
her up I secretly wished to put her down—she was so chubby.

Holding up my bangle to her, I say, 'Here, look at the
Makar heads. The two look the same. But does that mean the
beginning and the end are the same?'

Kuki busily returns to her homework, papers spread
all over the bed. Coming to Calcutta has meant she's had
to change schools—there's a different syllabus, the style of
teaching is different—these are not easy things for a ninth
grader to deal with in mid-session. Swapno wasn't too keen
on my coming to Calcutta. However, he has now finished
his M.Sc. and is ready to go to Kanpur; where we live is of
secondary interest to him. If he comes home, it'll be in the
long vacations. Ranjan still hasn't wound up the setup in
Swarupnagar—he's waiting for his Calcutta posting. Sirish
has just breathed relief after passing the exams for his B.Sc
in Geography. Now he's driving me crazy arguing about
whether he wants to be a photographer or work on a ship.
A certain wild, reckless, streak seems to be growing in him,
like a saal sapling. The system of education and exams, the
competition, nothing has been able to put a damper on this
unruly spirit of his.

From time to time, Stan shows up like a gust of wind.
Perhaps on his way to Delhi or Madras, passing through
Calcutta. He has travelled abroad twice in the last two
years—he was invited to conventions on human rights.
Stan's way of dressing has changed slightly; he doesn't wear
the Bengali-style dhoti-panjabi much any more. Instead, he
feels more comfortable in jeans and a khadi kurta. He hasn't
gained any weight at all, only the hair near the temples has

grayed; and when he skips shaving, kadam flowers bloom all over his cheeks. The moment he walks in the door, he falls on Sirish.

'You're spoiling him,' he says to me. 'The boy's becoming a babu-moshai. Very soon he'll forget about his own roots, won't even remember where he was born, in what home. Ei, Sirish, get ready, tomorrow you're going with me. I'm going to leave you in Bastar for a while. Work there for a year.'

Stan's organization has grown, in both size and structure. Bastar, Koraput and Dumka, they've opened new branches in these three places. That's where he wants to take Sirish.

Ranjan remarks, 'Sirish hasn't forgotten where he was born, his mother's the one who forgets.'

Amidst the collective laughter, I feel angry with Ranjan, and ashamed of the truth. While massaging coconut oil into Sirish's dry hair, I made a mistake and remarked, 'Ish-sh, the hair seems to be getting a bit thin in front! Maybe you're taking after your father.'

As Kuki broke into a giggle, and Ranjan too smiled, Sirish theatrically pretended to be rubbing his oil-smeared head on me and said, 'O Ammi, I've not taken after you, nor after Baba.'

It makes me a little sad when I think of that day. Ajay and Shyama went out for a picnic with their children with so much enthusiam. The picnic did not happen. In front of Kumardihi police station, the police had to throw tear gas shells and use lathis to disperse the crowd. Ajay did not allow shooting, even when an enraged crowd hit at them with brickbats, he himself was hit on the head and the back of his neck. Tirelessly he kept his forces restrained, turned angry like wounded tigers.

Stan was not arrested that day, nor was any case filed against him. If he were, the fire that would've started wouldn't have been easy to put out. To avoid complaint on the grounds of my knowing Stan, and hence any questions about my objectivity, I went away for the day, across the river to Jarangloi. Ranjan, Swapno and Kuki came with me. Later, Ajay said to me: 'The boy is capable all right! We only summoned him to the police station and people of nearly twenty villages got together within two hours. He must really have done something.'

Jhumur Tirki could not be found at her home that day; the man Ajayendra had sent to find her came back empty-handed after looking everywhere.

Jhumur's father was brought in completely drunk. The marks of beating on his body did not escape Ajayendra's eyes. Once this much was discovered, the M.L.A. backed out, saying, as any intelligent representative of the people would, 'I was talking on the basis of what Kumar Bahadur told me. Otherwise, nothing against D'Souza, you know, I've a special fondness for the boy.'

Outside, the people were still agitated. Ajayendra had informed them that no case would be filed until Jhumur herself gave a statement.

Angry Ranadeb threatened Ajayendra, citing the names of various ministers in the state capital. It didn't work. Finally, giving up, he tried to argue that Jhumur was a minor. That too didn't work. When he tried to leave town, Ajay stopped him: 'Don't leave now. Don't you see, how can things work if you leave? We're sending a force to Mahuldiha. They'll find Jhumur.' Two days later, Jhumur Tirki was found in semi-conscious state inside a hotel room in Mahuldiha. Despite severe beating, and close to real rape at the hands of

Ranadeb's mafia, she refused to write or sign an accusation of Stan.

The day all the volunteer organizations of the district gave Jhumur a reception for her courage, that very evening the transfer order reached Ajayendra's desk. The home minister did not agree that Ranadeb's arrest and swift charge- sheeting was urgent for the protection of human rights. Though neither M.L.A. nor M.P., Ranadeb was still the lifeblood of the party in Mahuldiha. And Ranadeb had made a counter-accusation, that Ajayendra had impudently come inside the palace, gun in hand and searched, not caring for 'Rani Anangamanjari's honour'.

Ajay came to say goodbye. He did not wait a moment after getting the order. He had let me know immediately, on the phone, of his decision to hand over charge. Shyama did not come with him. I understood, this proud woman simply couldn't forgive me. Instead of having a picnic in Chiri's saal forest, she was stuck for hours at the police station of Kumardihi, and had to face people hitting out at their car in fury, breaking its windows. What had hurt her the most was that Ajayendra was physically hit. Covering her children's eyes with her hands, she had watched, terrified, as stones were hurled at the window panes of the police station, smashing them to pieces. 'Shyama is still mad at me, isn't she Ajay?'

'Arre, don't worry about her. Her head will cool slowly. She's more upset about their sending me to some god-forsaken place. She asked me to appeal the order. How's that possible, tell me? Does a tiger ever eat grass out of hunger?'

Before leaving, as usual, he couldn't light a cigarette because there wasn't an ashtray. Shaking his head sadly, Ajayendra smiled. 'I give up, you won't change, ever. Oh well, tell me how you'll remember me. This whole year we spent just quarrelling.'

'Shall I say? Will you believe it?' I grew misty-eyed trying to say it. 'As the heroic fighter who ignored all temptation and fear, thinking of tears.'

'Wonderful!' His eyes danced in mock jest at the moment of leaving. 'If only I knew of this before, O my soulmate, I could've stayed on for a few more days!'

After Ajayendra and his family had left for Kumardihi police station, we set out to spend three wondrous days in Jarangloi. Ranjan and I with Swapno and Kuki. Three unreal days of sadness and joy mingling together. Ajayendra had given me his word. A total faith in this released me from all my worries. I wanted to leave the load of responsibilities at the turn of Khamarpara, cut my ties, and fly away. At the end of Aswin then, the river was about to start shrinking. In a few more days work would begin on the construction of the jetty. After that, at the close of winter, the fair-weather road would come up and completely change the scene. But before that happens, I wanted to show them the entrancing beauty of this flow of water. In morning light, in mid-day sun, under moonlight. The magical play, the lila of this river's many faces, with the shifting angle and changing quality of light.

I can't rest until I've shown Swapno and Kuki, where our 'Jalkanya' was docked, where I crossed the river, the spot where Bishai would swim up, the place where the three giant rocks slept. On the sandbar in the middle, I said, 'Look here, Swapno, look at these stones, I picked up some for you.'

Swapno was fascinated with the framework of the bridge. Even though there was no road, he wanted to climb the platform boards and find out how long it'd take to cross the river on foot. All that quite beyond Kuki, she was laughing, smearing herself with fistfuls of wet sand and dipping her hands and feet in the water.

Swapno wanted to meet Bishai Munda. I lost there. In fact, I last saw Bishai while crossing that very swollen river in Sravan. I still remember when he bit his tongue and swore on Ma Hangseswari as he put the few rupees I gave him into his waist-fold. Ramen took me to see Bishai Munda's sasandiri, his tombstone, in the burial ground on the riverbank, the barren stretch of burnt-out land where dead bodies of the Mundas, Lohras, Ghasis were buried. It was the only burial and cremation ground for Jarangloi and its three neighbouring panchayat areas. From what Ramen told me, I learnt that in the last three months as I was running around dealing with various events, Bishai's life changed in many ways. Any talk of the approach road made him angry and depressed. He simply couldn't accept the fact that the day the bridge was complete, even dogs and jackals would be walking across the river. And that the day was coming closer. Bishai's wife and children had left with a group migrating north to work in a brick kiln. That was at the beginning of Aswin, with the rains over, the skies clear, and the brick-kiln work about to start with the cool onset of Kartik.

As with the storybook's 'once a tiger got a bone in his throat…,' a bone got stuck in Bishai's throat one day. Of course it would be more appropriate to liken him to a little lamb than to a tiger. He probably hadn't had good food in ages. That's why at duskfall one day, after long sweating labour, he was ravenously hungry when the food came. Early morning that day in mid-Aswin, drums had sounded through the villages under Jarangloi's tribal panchayat. The bhandari

was announcing that the sasandiri of Hukum Munda, a
bigwig of Kalikapur village, was going to be carried that day.
The Munda community follows the custom of placing a big
stone upright on the grave as memorial. The more eminent
the man, the bigger the stone. People are needed to carry it.
All strong men under the panchayat ran with bamboo, ropes
and crowbars to answer the call. Bishai too joined, mainly for
the feast that was to follow. Hukum Munda was tight-fisted,
even though he had a lot of land, and it turned out that his two
sons Anik and Tura were like their father. Nearly a hundred
men had responded to the call, yet Anik and Tura wanted to
get away with two sheep and two goats. Anik pleaded that he
couldn't afford more; the group's leader Mukhan threatened
(mostly mock, of course) that not one of them would help him
bury his father if he was going to be so stingy. Finally, Tura
procured two more goats and saved his brother's honour. But
all this negotiation had taken up some time. After setting the
huge stone upright in the ground, doing the worship rites,
and bathing in the river, when they finally sat down to eat,
twilight was falling thick on the riverside.

That meal was the end of Bishai. He thought a goat bone
had got lodged in his throat. His throat became swollen,
infected, and so painful that Bishai couldn't even drink water,
let alone have any food or his toddy. Everybody kept scaring
him to get him to go and see a doctor. Scared to die without
his alcohol, Bishai ran everywhere like an animal on fire. First,
to Jarangloi's health centre, where he waited for two days at
the door, because the doctor was absent. The 'compounder',
whom he begged for help, pointed to the out-of-order X-ray
machine and advised him to go to Khamarpara. The doctor
in Khamarpara was unnerved by what he saw and advised
him to go to Kumardihi. Taking a minute to write a reference

letter, he said: 'Looks like you'll need surgery. The company hospital there has sophisticated instruments.' Admission in Kumardihi's company hospital, he was told, involved a cash payment of four hundred rupees. Borrowing the money took Bishai another two days. No one had given him the vital information that with the help of the Red Cross, he could get free treatment there. His skin-and-bones frame in a dirty lungi did not make it to the operation table.

Uma Samanta told me, the reason his throat was so swollen came out in the X-ray report. 'You know what it was? A piece of iron wire an inch and a half long. Not a bone. It was mixed in the rice. He was eating in the dark…bad luck.'

This bone or wire that stuck in his throat raised very many questions. At least Swapno asked many, which I haven't quite been able to answer to this day. Why was there no doctor at Jarangloi? Why didn't the X-ray machine work? Why did admission at the company hospital cost money? Why the delay in the surgery even after admission? And above all, when was the bridge going to be ready? How much longer would the people on this side of the river have to run in sickness to Khamarpara, to Kumardihi? No, Swapno didn't quite put his questions so clearly, he was too young for that. But if what he said was properly arranged, it would sound just this way. The part that was withheld from Swapno was about how Gagan Mahato the creditor was planning to recover the four hundred rupee loan he gave Bishai from Bishai's wife, once the brick-kiln season was over.

Bishai's sasandiri was small. He didn't have money, no pots and pans, no sheep and goats, not a thing. About four men from his village got together to set up a small stone, perform a token worship, take a token bite, and went home after washing their feet in the river. Standing in the shadow of twilight, Ranjan, Swapno, Kuki and I placed some flowers at the sasandiri. Swapno's pockets were filled with coloured pebbles. These he set out there, in a nice arrangement. Uma Samanta and Ramen were absolutely silent. Ramen suddenly said, 'In a way it's better, Bishai didn't live to see the bridge finished, his spirit will rest in peace.'

From the river's edge, we were walking carefully up the muddy bank, towards Jarangloi. Ranjan, a tired Kuki in his arms, walking ahead with Uma-babu. Swapno and I a little way behind. Holding my little finger in his hand, Swapno said in a carefully lowered voice, 'Ma, you know what? I know about everything. Baba has told me.'

There was a tremor of fear inside my chest. How had Ranjan put it to him?

Lifting his beaming face to me, Guddu then said: 'Baba is Kuki's father, but you're my mother, Kuki's too…. Baba said—Sirish is going to come next month. He doesn't have his father, his mother, anyone. We'll all live together then. Like this.' Swapno jingled the pebbles in his pocket.

After walking some distance, I turned back and looked at the dark river. Some time earlier the moon had appeared, reddish and angry, atop the forest. Now its placid face shone like a well-scrubbed brass plate, its reflection in the water shivering in different ways before blending away.

The black water rolled over everything, sending out its wrenching call, the sleeping pale sandbar in the middle. The landing ghat was visible hazily, from where we stood. And the dim light of the ghat.

That was really the last time I saw the river.